"Do you even know what day it is?" Ali asked. "How difficult this is?"

She whirled to walk into the house, but Jericho captured her arm and made her face him. Setting the basket down, he placed his hands on her shoulders. "Today is the nine-year anniversary of the day the girl of my dreams married me. It was the happiest day of my life. I could never forget."

Tears made her eyes look like melted chocolate. His gut twisted. He never wanted to be the cause for this woman crying ever again.

"Your anniversary gift is in there on the table."

"My gift?"

He smiled. "I owe you a heap more. I'll make up for the lost years, too, if you'll let me."

JESSICA KELLER

As a child, Jessica possessed the dangerous combination of too much energy coupled with an overactive imagination. This pairing led to more than seven broken bones and countless scars. Oddly enough, she's worked as a zookeeper, librarian, camp counselor, horse wrangler, housekeeper and finance clerk, but now loves her full-time work in law enforcement. Former editor of both her college newspaper and literary journal at Trinity International University, Jessica received degrees in both Communications and Biblical Studies. She lives in the Chicagoland suburbs with her amazing husband and two annoyingly outgoing cats who also happen to be named after superheroes.

Home for Good
Jessica Keller

Love Inspired

Recycling programs
for this product may
not exist in your area.

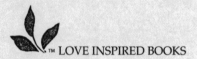

™ LOVE INSPIRED BOOKS

ISBN-13: 978-0-373-87797-3

HOME FOR GOOD

www.LoveInspiredBooks.com

Printed in U.S.A.

Hope deferred makes the heart sick,
but a longing fulfilled is a tree of life.
—*Proverbs* 13:12

Thank you to Mom and Dad, for all your support. To Lisa, who always believed in me. The Wunderlich sisters, who were never shy about feedback, and for both being as in love with Jericho as I am. Special kudos goes to Sadie who urged me to write in the first place. Thanks George and Wanda, for taking the time to answer all my questions about living in the country. Carol and Kristy, my beloved NovelSisters, your prayers made this book a reality. And to Matthew, I could never express in words how much your support and encouragement means to me. I love you so much.

Chapter One

After what seemed like a lifetime of bad days, Ali Silver couldn't wait to share a carefree afternoon with her son at the city picnic. Sunshine washed through the valley, giving a glow to the rivers and casting shadows out of the sharp mountain canyons to the west. With the pickup's windows rolled down, the air drifted in, spiced with alfalfa and silver sage. Fields of bucking hay splashed across the landscape, juxtaposed with the occasional lone apple tree—relics left-over from once substantial orchards.

Ali drove with one hand on the wheel, the other cocked in the open window. "Hang on to that. We don't want to spill it before the soldiers get to taste it."

Her son, Chance, hugged the bowl on his lap. "I know. This is the special potato salad. The one you only make for special people."

"Like you." She winked at him.

After waiting in a line of traffic to enter the park, Ali ma-neuvered her beast of a truck into one of the last available spots. She took the potato salad from Chance, and they am-bled toward the crowd near the food tables. A couple local firefighters manned the grills. They waved. The smell of siz-zling brats tickled her nose.

Hannah, a shop owner in town, signaled to Ali. "Isn't this just the nicest thing? I do believe the Hamilton Civic Club pulled out all the stops to honor these troops."

Ali balanced the bowl against her hip. "Having a picnic to honor the local servicemen who have returned this year was a great idea. I'm glad the town is doing something. And Chance loves anything to do with the army, so he's tickled to meet them."

Hannah clasped her hands together. "Oh, yes. I like them teaching the young people to support the troops."

Chance yanked on Ali's arm.

Hannah chuckled. "That boy's eager!"

Messing up his hair, Ali smiled down at her son. "Go on and find Aunt Kate and see if you can snag an empty table for us."

Without waiting to hear more, Chance took off running. Ali's heart squeezed. He might mirror her brown-sugar-like freckles, but the thick maple-colored hair that stuck up on the side when he woke in the morning, his square jaw, the angular nose and intense pale blue eyes—all of that belonged to his father. Chance looked just like...

Ali shook her head. She did not want to think about *him*. Not today. Not ever.

Instead she chose to weave through groups of mingling neighbors, greeting them with a nod since her hands were full. She located an empty place for the potato salad on a table already loaded with deviled eggs, baked beans and desserts. Satisfied that the food situation was under control, Ali snatched a gooey-looking brownie and raised it to her lips.

"Hiya, Ali."

The voice from her past rocketed through her with the force of a kick drum. The brownie flew out of her hand, leaving a powdered-sugar trail down her shirt on its way to the hard dirt. She spun around.

Jericho Freed.

All six feet of him, clad in jeans and a fitted gray-striped button-down. His bold, masculine eyebrows rose as he surveyed her with look-me-in-the-eyes-if-you-dare blues. He wore a straw cowboy hat with unruly hair poking out, and a five o'clock shadow outlined his firm jaw. More than eight years later, and the man still made her mouth go dry.

It frustrated her that after everything, he still had that power.

So she did the only rational thing she could think to do. *Flee.*

In a fluid movement, Ali sidestepped him and took off sprinting at a breakneck clip. Her hat flew off.

He yelled out her name.

And just like in the past, his voice poured sweet and velvety, like chocolate over each syllable. Ali's nails dug into her palms. She didn't want to hear him. She never wanted to fall under his spell again. Tears gathered at the corners of her eyes as she ran.

Why was he here? Oh, why hadn't she moved away when she had the…chance? *Chance!* Suddenly she pounded faster, the narrow toe of her boots chafing against her feet.

Jericho couldn't see Chance. She wouldn't let that happen. *God, please!*

Ali zeroed in on her sister Kate milling next to the volleyball court.

She waved her arms. "Quick! We have to find Chance! Now!" Ali pressed a hand to the stitch in her side as she looked over her shoulder, scanning the crowd for the cowboy with impossibly blue eyes. He hadn't followed her.

Kate jogged toward Ali, her eyes wide. "Sis? I don't see smoke coming from your hair, so if it's not on fire—what is?"

She seized Kate's arms, clamping down on reality. "He's

here. He's back. What am I supposed to… What if he… What about Chance?" Her voice rose in a frenzy.

Kate shook her gently. "Who's here?"

"My husband."

"Ali! Alison!" With his hands looped onto his belt buckle, Jericho kicked, sending a cloud of Montana dust into the air. Maybe he should chase after her, but his knees probably couldn't handle running at that clip.

Great. Just great.

He rubbed the back of his neck as Ali hightailed it like a spooked filly. At that speed, she might make the Canadian border by nightfall. It sure wasn't funny, though. A man couldn't laugh, not when the rejection felt like a sledgehammer hitting him square in the chest. The cold look in her hazel eyes told him where he stood. Unwelcome. Unforgiven. How could he have expected anything else? But her reaction rankled him all the same.

He rubbed his jaw and growled. Could he blame her? No. What kind of man envisions a warm welcome after eight years of silence? Jericho Eli Freed. *Stupid man.*

A young boy with floppy hair ambled toward him. "Are you really a soldier?"

Jericho cleared his throat, pulled at the fabric of his army pants and dropped to one knee. "I sure am." Or was.

"That's cool. I want to be a soldier someday." At this confession, the child looked down and dug his toe into the ground.

Keeping his voice low to draw the kid out of his shell, Jericho asked, "Do you feel funny around new people? 'Cause I sure do. When I was your age, I just had one friend in the world and she was the only person I'd talk to." Jericho laid a hand on the boy's scrawny shoulder.

Suddenly a shadow loomed over them. "Get your hands off of him."

Jericho jerked back and looked up—and his mouth fell open. Fire in her eyes, Ali Silver stood there, an arm wrapped around the boy as she pulled him close.

Jericho jumped to his feet, putting his hands palm up in surrender.

Even seething mad, beauty radiated from her. Sure, she had changed in the last eight years, but in a good way. Auburn mellowed her once fire-truck-red hair. The long tresses he remembered were now cut so they skimmed her ears. Cute.

Ali. His Ali. She'd been a slim thing, barely entering womanhood when he left. Now she had gentle curves that he had to school his eyes not to explore. Her hazel eyes held a soft sincerity that drew him in. A familiar tightening gripped his stomach as his pulse started to go berserk.

The kid pushed against her. "No, Mom, he's not a stranger. This is a soldier. We were becoming friends."

Jericho's mind raced like a mouse caught in a maze. *Mom?* The single word sent a zap through his body, like someone had dumped a vat of ice over his head. Ali was a mother? Had she remarried? Impossible. The kid was what? Six? Seven—?

"Ali?" He tried to meet her gaze, but she looked away.

"Hey, Chance." Ali leaned over to speak close to the child's ear. "I think I see your teacher, Mrs. McBride, over there. Can you do me a favor and find out how she liked those pies we made her?"

"Ali?" Jericho repeated. His mind latched onto the name *Chance* and filed it away for later.

Chance's brow creased. He looked at Jericho, then back at his mother. "How come he knows your name, Mom?"

Despite the sweltering day, a cold sweat pricked the back of Jericho's neck.

Her mouth went dry. No matter what, Ali had to get Chance away from Jericho. She placed her hands on her hips. "It doesn't matter, Chance. Now go visit with Mrs. McBride for a minute." After sending Chance away, she took a deep breath and turned to address Jericho, but couldn't make herself completely meet his gaze. "I don't know why you're here—"

"We need to talk." He shoved his hands into his pockets.

"There is no 'we.'"

He quirked an eyebrow. "I disagree. Unless I slept through signing some sort of papers, you and I, well, we're still married."

Her tongue suddenly felt like a dried-up riverbed. *We're still married.* Fear skittered down her spine like racing spiders. Of course. As a teen mom on her own, she didn't have spare money to toss around on lawyer fees.

She balled up her fists. "I want you to leave."

He shook his head, reached a hand out toward her, then dropped it to his side. "I'm back, Ali—back for good."

"Why?" The word came out more whisper than force.

She stared into his intense blue eyes, her gaze dipping to the single freckle above his lip. Same dime-sized scar near his eye, the slight tug of his lips—always ready to joke.

He stepped closer. "I need to talk to you. Explain about being away."

"Just *being away?* How nice. Sounds warm and fuzzy, like you took a vacation."

He ran a hand over his hair, cupping the back of his neck as he tipped his head to the side. "I always wanted to come back. But—"

"Stay away from me. Stay away from my son."

"I need to—" He reached for her.

She slapped away his hand.

"Ali..." He grabbed her elbow, and a thrill skittered up her arm and down into her stomach. She let out a muffled cry. Why? Why, after all these years, was his name still branded across her heart?

Fighting the hot tears stinging her eyes, she jerked from him. "Don't touch me. Please, don't touch me." A sob hung at the back of her throat. "I can't do this. I can't handle being this close. I can't talk to you."

"But I have to talk to you. Give me fifteen minutes. Please?" His voice flowed, soft and reassuring.

"No!" She swiped at the traitorous tears squeezing from her eyes.

A warm, steady hand touched the small of her back. She turned to find Tripp Phillips, local lawyer, old classmate and friend, beside her. In his usual dress pants and polo, his stability brought an ease of calm to her shaking nerves. She gripped his arm.

"Alison, is something wrong?" Tripp's voice came out controlled and comforting. He had a manner that made even the most skeptical of strangers immediately warm to him. "Is Freed bothering you?"

"Tripp Phillips, I don't believe you were a part of our conversation." Jericho's voice hardened.

"Rightly so, but I'm not going to stand around while you make Alison cry."

"I'm not crying," Ali mumbled.

Tripp turned her into his shoulder. His hand cradled the back of her head as he wedged his body between her and Jericho.

Jericho growled.

Chance chose that moment to come bounding back. "What's wrong, Mom?" He wrapped his arm around Ali's waist and peered at her from under thick black eyelashes. "Mrs. McBride liked the pies, but I didn't tell her about the green worms we found in the berries. Did you think I did? Is that why you're crying?"

"I'm not upset about the worms, honey." Ali caressed his tanned face, and Chance rewarded her with an impish grin.

Tripp cleared his throat. "I think your mom's not feeling well today, buddy. We better take her home."

Jericho held her gaze. "Ali, I'm not done trying to talk to you."

Tripp turned and led her away from the monster of her past. Good old Tripp. At least one dependable man remained. If only Tripp had been the one to chase her in high school instead of Jericho, life might have turned out differently. At least Tripp stood by her now, always helping and advising her. His sound counsel lifted a weight from her shoulders, and she was grateful.

Chance twisted around, then cupped his hands around his mouth. "Wait! Are you going to be at the fireworks show tonight?"

A chill ran through her veins.

Then that voice from her dreams over the last eight years answered back. "'Course, Chance. I wouldn't miss it for the world."

Jericho wanted to hit something. No, he wanted a drink. A nice, tall amber malt with a high head of foam. Hadn't wanted that for five years, but there you go.

Looping a hand over the back of his neck, Jericho tensed as Tripp guided Ali away, like an auctioneer showing off a prized mare.

Could Tripp be Chance's father? Fear sliced through him.

Jericho stalked past the picnic and grabbed the door handle on the rusted Jeep he had found at his dad's house. So she ran into another man's arms when he left? And if he was right about the kid's age, she didn't even wait for sunset before finding comfort in Tripp.

He kicked the tire.

Maybe he had left Ali, but he'd always been faithful. Always loved Ali, and only Ali. Left because he loved her too much to stay and watch himself destroy her.

Jericho climbed into the vehicle and slammed the door. He closed his eyes and pinched the bridge of his nose. What was a man to do? He came home to mend his marriage. After all his wandering, Jericho finally felt like a man worthy of being a husband.

Was he too late?

Chapter Two

As Ali drove under the American flags suspended above Main Street, panic welled up in her throat.

She'd have to see *him.*

"Mom, drive faster. We're gonna be late to the fireworks." Chance bounced in the backseat.

From the passenger's seat, her sister Kate laid a hand on Ali's arm. "Are you all right?"

Ali glanced back at her son. "This traffic's pretty bad."

Kate shrugged. "Everyone is just excited. A week ago we thought the show would be canceled like last year."

"I still can't believe the donations the city got at the last minute. Wish I knew who had purse strings like that. I could tap them for Big Sky Dreams." Ali bit her lip. The worry she felt over the financial problems of her nonprofit organization was never far from her mind.

"This is different. The Fourth of July. People get excited about patriotic stuff."

"You think blowing up a bunch of cardboard is more important than helping handicapped kids?"

"Now don't go putting words in my mouth, big sis. You know I think what you do is worthwhile. I'm just saying, the draw for something like this is more universal."

Ali bumped the truck along the grass-trodden lot being used to park overflow for the fireworks show. The three climbed out, scooped up their blankets and plodded across the fairground's field, looking for a spot to claim. Ali stopped often to chat with her neighbors, wave to her horseback-riding students and embrace folks she'd grown up with.

As the first explosion resounded in the sky, Ali relaxed. Propped on her elbows, she laid back, watching her son's face more than the Fourth of July display. His mouth hung slack as his eyes sparkled to match the show lighting up the night sky. He wore a giant toothy grin. She wished she could recapture that feeling in her own life. Would she ever again know that feeling of freedom, of trusting and letting go? Where had her joy gone?

Jericho Eli Freed. That's where. The man had successfully smashed her hope of a white knight when he ran off like a bandit with her dreams.

Standing there, ten feet away from the love of his life, watching her smile and sigh, an ache filled Jericho that reached clear to his toes. So his Ali wasn't all mountain lion snarls and rattlesnake warnings. As she watched her son, softness filled her face. *Beautiful.* Staring at his wife, his mind blanked out.

"Hey, lover-boy." A warm hand touched his arm, and he glanced over. Kate stood at his elbow. "Are you going to look at her all night? Or will you man up and do something?"

"You're talking to me? I figured all the Silvers hated my guts."

Kate motioned for him to follow her a few paces away from where Ali and Chance sat. She dropped her voice to a whisper. "Are you still in love with my sister?"

Jericho swallowed hard. *Bold little thing.* The last time he'd seen Kate, she'd been a skinned-knee kid.

"Well? Answer me, cowboy." Her eyebrow drove higher.

Jericho cleared his throat. "Yes. 'Course. I've always loved her, always will."

Kate nodded. "Bingo. Well, if that's the case, I'll help you."

"You wanna help me get Ali back?"

She let out a long stream of air, like he was daft for not tracking with the conversation. "Yes. When you left, Ali fell to pieces. You know better than anyone that she didn't have the easiest life. But with you, when you were there for her, all that other stuff didn't strangle her. Then you left, and…"

You destroyed her.

"I know. I'm sorry. I'd do anything to change the fact that I left."

"But I need to know, before we become partners in this, are you a better man now?" She jammed a finger into his chest, and he knew exactly what she meant. *You still a drunk? Ornery? Will you leave again?*

He lifted his hands, palms out. "I'm a man surrendered now, Kate. Still make mistakes. But I haven't touched a bottle in five years, and I've made a promise to God that I never will. I won't hurt Ali. I came back to make good on my wedding vows…to honor and protect her, to fix what I did. But she doesn't want me at all."

"I think you're wrong."

"But what about Chance?"

Kate held up a hand and shook her head. "Not my story to tell."

Sweat slicked his palms. "Don't know, Kate. I was watching her just now. She smiles for everyone but me. She started crying when I talked to her. I think she'd relish watching the buzzards pecking at me before seeing me again."

"That's because if she lets down her guard with you, she stands to lose the most."

"Meaning?"

"You cowboys are all seriously dense."

He rolled his eyes. "Continue."

"She's closed off to you because she loves you the most. That makes you the biggest danger of all. If someone else rejects her or betrays her, she can shrug that off, but you? That's everything to her. Has been since you two were kids."

Well, that was clear as mud.

"So here's the plan." She glanced back at Ali, then leaned toward him. "In a minute these fireworks will be done, and I'm going to ferret away Chance with the lure of some sparklers." She patted the bulge in her purse. "That'll leave you a good amount of time to talk to Ali."

"But what do I say?"

"If you can't figure that out, cowboy, then you don't deserve my sister."

Alone, lying back and scanning the night sky through the leftover smoke hanging in the air, Ali almost breathed a thankful sigh—but then *he* sat down next to her, took off his hat and tapped the brim against his leg.

"I don't want you—"

"I know." He wound his hat around in his hands, and the motion tugged at all the broken places inside her. "I know you don't want me. And after a time, if you still feel that way, I'll honor that. I'll leave you alone for good."

"Good, I want that. Now." She started to sit up, gathering the blanket Chance and Kate shared during the show, but his warm hand on her arm stopped her. He gently turned her to face him.

She sighed. "Okay, if I let you talk, we'll be done? You'll leave after that?"

"If that's really what you want." He ran his fingers over the rim of his hat.

"It is. So go ahead, shoot."

He gave the slightest sign of an outlaw smile. "Not a good thing to say to a cowboy."

She rolled her eyes. "Speak, rover. Talk. Say whatever it is you're so bent on telling me."

He shifted. "I should have never left."

"You've got that right."

He placed a hand on her arm and gently squeezed. "Let me talk, woman, please." Jericho removed his hand. "That day. You've got to understand that I had to go. I had no choice. I was so afraid that I'd hurt you, Ali. I loved you so much, and I sat there watching myself destroy the one person in the world who meant anything to me. That day when I lost it… tossed your lamp…well, I saw a streak of my pop in me, and it made me sick. I got in my car and just took off, kicking up a cloud of dust."

Blinking the burn away from her eyes, Ali moved to stand up. "I don't need to hear a replay of this. In case you forgot, I was there."

He stopped her with a touch of his hand. "Please stay."

Who was he to beg her to stay? But like a fool, she hunkered back down.

"I stopped at Pop's house and had an all-out yelling brawl with him, then lit for the state line. I got a job driving a tour bus at Yellowstone. They canned me a couple months later when they found out I hit the scotch before the rides. I spent the next year or two working as a ranch hand at different places, most of the time herding at the back, eating cattle dust and that's about all I felt I was good for. I thought about coming back—wanted to—but I was a sorry mess that you didn't need. I drank more than before. Drank all my money away. But God kept me alive, so I could come back to you and—"

"I hardly think God has anything to do with it. You were a drunk, lying, good-for-nothing boy."

He nodded. "I can't argue you about that. I was. And I took the coward's way. I just needed—" he closed his eyes "—escape."

Ali bit back a stream of words. Adults didn't get the choice of escape. They bucked up and dealt with it, like she had. "Escape from what? Me?" Her muscles cringed. *Never enough.* Her love couldn't heal him. She'd failed as a wife, and that's why he left.

"No. Never you. I needed to escape *me.*" He thumbed his chest. "I was furious at God for taking my mom, hated Pop for becoming a cruel drunk—then hated myself just as much for becoming everything I despised in him. I was angry that I couldn't be what you needed. I talked you into running away from your family in the middle of the night, into marrying me when you were only eighteen. I had nothing to give you but my heap of troubles. I was just a kid myself, and I didn't have the first clue how to take care of you properly. What kind of man was I? So I drank. I wanted to be numb. I wanted nothing to matter anymore, but I kept seeing your face, kept catching whiffs of pretty flowers that reminded me of you." His ratty straw hat flaked apart as he twisted it round and round in his hands while talking.

With a bull-rider's grip on her purse, Ali chewed her bottom lip. Jericho's humility unnerved her. He was supposed to be cocky. He was supposed to smell of alcohol, combined with the cigar smoke from whatever bar he'd rolled out of at three in the morning. But no, he sat here emitting an intoxicating mixture of hard work, rain and alfalfa.

He paused, his soft eyes studying her. When she didn't respond, he continued. "It got worse, though. I found myself sneaking into barns at night just for a place to sleep away the hangover. Homeless…can you imagine?" He gave a humorless laugh. "The great ranch baron Abram Freed's son, homeless." He threw up his hands. "One night an old rancher found me, and I thought he was going to shoot me between the eyes, but he invited me inside. Let me sleep in his guest bedroom. He was a veteran, and when he talked about his time in the service he just became a hero to me. This man had been through so much terrible stuff, but he was even-keeled and kind. And I wanted to be him. So I enlisted. I owe that man the life I have now."

"You're really a soldier, then?"

He put back on his hat, steepling his hands together. "Ali, who's Chance's dad?"

The question froze every inch of her that had thawed during his story. "He doesn't have one. He's *my* son. That's it."

"Unless he's adopted…that's not really possible."

"Are you done?" She knew her harsh tone would wound his open spirit, but she didn't care. Not when Chance got pulled into the conversation.

He sighed and worked the kinks out of the back of his neck. "After I enlisted, I went through training and spent some good time learning what it means to be a man of discipline and determination. After a couple years my group got drawn for deployment, and I wanted to call you, wanted to say goodbye, but didn't feel like I had the right to. Not one person I cared about knew I was over there, knew I could die at any minute."

Die? Her head snapped up. Could he have died without her ever knowing? Wouldn't her heart have felt the loss? Regardless of her anger, she would never have wanted that.

Across the field, Kate and Chance picked their way toward her.

"…but then one day we were sent on this mission and—"

She cut him off. "That's great, Jericho. Sounds like life without us worked out just fine for you. Our lives have been good without you, too. I got some schooling and started a nonprofit that I really care about." She rose, hoping he'd follow suit.

"Without us?" He took the blankets from her arms.

"What?" Her tongue raced against the back of her teeth.

He quirked both eyebrows. "You said *us,* plural."

She pushed him away with her best glare. "Us…as in the Bitterroot Valley, your dad, the people here in Montana that you grew up with." Her hands shook. Almost gave it away. Foolish mouth.

Chance's rapid steps approached.

"Your story, well, it doesn't change much for me. I still want you to turn on those boots and do that walking-out bit you're so good at."

"I can't, Ali, not yet."

"But you said you'd leave if that's what I wanted, and I do."

"I came back because I have to ask your forgiveness. And if we can, I want to fix our marriage. Be there for you like I promised nine years ago."

"I don't want that."

"Hey, Mom! You found Jericho!" Chance frolicked around the two adults.

"How were the sparklers, buddy?" She dropped down and pulled her son into her arms.

Chance's gaze flew to Jericho, and his cheeks colored. The little imp wiggled free. "They were great. My friend Michael told this girl Samantha that he was going to put a sparkler in her hair and light it on fire. But Kate told him that someday he'll be sorry he ever talked to girls that way."

"I'm sure he will be." Still on her knees, she smiled.

Chance turned toward Jericho. "You're a guy. What do you think?"

"I think your mom and your aunt are right. A real man is always nice to a girl." His gaze locked on Ali. "Always."

Chance grabbed Jericho's sleeve, pulling the man to his level. "Were you talking to my mom again? Do you know her?"

Ali jumped in. "Jericho and I did know each other, but it was a really long time ago, pal. His dad's ranch backs up to ours. We were neighbors."

Chance took her hand. "That's cool, so we can share him."

Behind him, Kate attempted to hide a laugh with a cough.

"Hey, Jericho, it's my birthday in two days. Will you

come to my party? Looks like you already know where our house is."

"Chance! Did you ever think Jericho might have other things to do with his time?" Ali's eyes widened. *Please let Jericho have something to do that day.*

Jericho spread out his arms and let a low, rumbling laugh escape his lips. "I'll be there, champ. I'm free."

"Then will you promise to teach me to ride a ewe?" The child's eyes lit up, hands clasped together.

Jericho rose. He rubbed his jaw and looked to Ali. She shook her head. "I think you're too big for mutton bustin'. The kids who do that are five or six."

Chance crossed his arms. "It's not fair. Our ranch hand, Rider, won't teach me. Now you won't, either."

"I could teach you something else. How about roping? Do you know how to lasso a steer? 'Cause that's loads harder than riding sheep."

"You promise you'll come teach me?"

"I'll bring the dummy steer and everything." Jericho smiled down at Ali's son, and her heart squeezed—with panic or tenderness, though, she couldn't be sure. One thing she knew—Jericho Freed was back in her life, whether she wanted him there or not.

Chapter Three

Scientific research said mint-and-tan-painted walls were supposed to soothe her, but each step Ali took toward her mother's room weighed her down like shuffling through deep mud. She nodded to other residents of the facility as they teetered down the hallway, gripping the railing that ran waist-level throughout the nursing home. She clutched her purse against her stomach. Mom didn't belong here. People in their fifties shouldn't be stuck like this.

Paces away from Mom's door, Ali leaned against the wall and sucked in a fortifying breath. It stung her throat with the artificial smells of bleach and cafeteria food. She pulled the paper out of her purse and read it again.

I saw you together at the Independence Day picnic. If you value what's important to you, you'll stay away from him. You've been warned.

Ali didn't know whether she should run to the police department or laugh. The glued-on magazine letters looked straight out of a cheesy television crime show. But was the threat serious? Who would leave such a thing tacked to her front door? Thankfully, her head ranch hand, Rider, found it before Chance woke up. Her son could pretend bravado, but with something like this, he would have dissolved into a puddle of tears.

She racked her mind, tallying a list of the people she remembered seeing at the picnic yesterday. Not one of them would have cared in the least if they saw her speaking with Jericho. Who wanted to keep them apart? Not that she minded. That's what she wanted anyway, right? All the more reason to steer clear of the man, but it grated to be threatened.

Unless… No, it couldn't be. Abram Freed had never been fond of his son's attachment to her, but she'd made her peace with the cantankerous cowboy years after Jericho left. Besides, with the paralysis on the right side of his body, the man couldn't move—he lay in a bed here in the same nursing home as her mother. He couldn't harm her, and he'd keep her secret about Chance, too.

A nurse wearing a teal smock broke into her thoughts. "You gonna go in and say howdy to your ma?"

"Hi, Sue. How's Mom doing today?"

The nurse's blond eyebrow rose. "No disrespect, but your ma's the most ornery patient we have. But we don't mind none. She's a fighter at that. I think most people would be gone already with what she's got, but she just keeps hanging right on."

Ali gave a tight-lipped smile. "She's a handful."

Jamming the menacing letter back into her purse, she smoothed down her shirt and ran a hand over her hair before entering her mother's room. The sight of Marge Silver—weak with pale skin hanging in long droops off her arms and a map of premature wrinkles covering her face as she whistled air in and out through the oxygen nosepiece—always made Ali's knees shake a little bit.

"How you feeling, Ma?" She came to the side of the bed. Ali felt a deep emptiness. Her mom's eyes stared back, cold and hopeless. Shut off, like her spirit had already given up.

"Dying... Been better." The words wheezed out, stilting every time the oxygen infused.

Ali crossed her arms and buried her balled-up fists deep in her armpits. She wanted to take her mother's hand in both of hers, but she knew better. Never one to show affection, her mother wouldn't have considered the touch comforting. "You aren't dying."

"Want to.... Nothing left...here."

"You know that's not true. There is Kate and me and Chance."

"Not that any of...you...care."

"I wouldn't be here if I didn't care, and I know Kate visited just the other day."

"The ranch?"

Ali straightened a vase on the bedside table. "It's fine."

"The...lawsuit?"

Ali bit her lip. She should be used to this by now; her mom asked the same questions every time she visited. But somehow, the little girl in Ali who wanted to know her mom loved her came with expectations that left her drifting in an ocean of hurt every time. Besides, she didn't want to think about the deaths of that poor couple. It was an accident.

"Don't worry about that. Tripp's taking care of it. He always does the best for us."

"Has to.... None of the rest of you...have any thought... in your heads. Never...happen...if your father...still alive."

Ali pulled her purse tighter up on her shoulder, then gripped the bed rails. "I miss Daddy too, Ma."

"Your fault...he's dead."

"Don't say that."

"So...selfish, had...to ride. Had...to...rodeo."

"It's hardly my fault Dad got caught under that bull's hooves." Ali stared out the window, fanning her face with her hand to dry the tears clinging to her eyelids. She tried to block out the memory of her dad, the amateur rider Buck Silver, being crushed again and again by two thousand pounds of angry muscle and horns. She saw his body go limp, remembered trying to run into the arena but Jericho's strong arms held her back.

"Your fault…men leave. Your dad…your husband."

"You're wrong. Jericho's back," Ali ground out.

"If he finds…out. He'll…take your son. You'll…be alone."

"He doesn't know about Chance, and he has no reason to ever know."

"People…always leave."

"That doesn't have to be true. Chance will always be with me. And Kate's back right now."

"How long…before she goes…too?"

"I don't know, Mom. Here, I brought you some stuff from the house." Ali set a bunched paper bag on the nightstand. "I'll see you next week."

Ali barreled out of the doorway—and straight into Jericho Freed's solid chest.

"Whoa, there." Jericho grabbed Ali's slender biceps to steady her.

"I'm not a horse." She jerked away.

"Of course you're not." He tipped her chin with his finger, and her red-rimmed eyes, tears carving twin paths down either side of her face, made his stomach flip. "Why are you crying?"

She swiped her face with the back of her hand. "What are you doing here?"

"Pop."

"Oh, I knew that. I'm sorry. It was so sad—he was all alone. They aren't sure how long he lay there…"

"You're avoiding my question." He gave a smile he hoped exuded safety and reassurance. "Why the tears?"

She tossed her hands in the air. "Oh, just another invigorating talk with my mother."

"She's here, too?"

Ali shrugged and gave an unflattering grimace in what looked like an attempt to hold back emotion. "She has lung cancer. I mean, we should have expected it. She smoked three or four packs every day of my life, and only got worse after we lost Dad."

"And let me take a guess—she's still as bitter and mean as ever."

Ali met his gaze, and the tears brought out the gold flecks in her eyes. For a moment he couldn't breathe. "She's had a hard life."

"True, but she doesn't have to take it out on you. Don't blame her moods on yourself. It's fully her choice how she treats people."

"You're one to talk," she mumbled and he swallowed a growl.

Could she never forgive him?

He blocked her path when she moved to walk around him. "Are you going to be all right?"

She dug her toe into the floor, and in a small voice confessed, "She still blames me for killing Dad."

He wanted to scoop her up in his arms and feel her head resting against his chest, trusting his strength as he carried her away from all the people who tried to tie millstones around her neck. Quashing that desire, he settled for cupping her elbow and leading her outside, away from the oppression and doom of the nursing home. Thankfully, she walked right along with him, even leaned into his touch a little bit.

When they got outside, he led her to her truck then turned her to face him. He rested his hands on her shoulders. His blues met her sparkling hazels as he said in a soft, low voice, "It wasn't your fault. Your dad made a choice that day to get on that bull. He took a risk, and it turned out to be a disastrous one. But that's all it was, an accident."

She worked that bottom lip between her teeth. "But he

would have been trucking. He wouldn't have been at the rodeo if I hadn't been so bent on barrel racing."

"He loved the rodeo. I'm just sorry we were there to see it that day."

Ali nodded in an absent way, then pushed up on his wrists. Jericho let go of her, but as he stepped back he noticed something curious. "Your tires are on their rims."

"What? I just drove here. They were fine." Ali turned around and then slapped her hand over her mouth.

Jericho bent down to examine the tires. Sure enough, each one bore a deep slash. Intentional. His stomach rolled. "Cut. Know why someone would want to make mincemeat of your tires?"

She dragged in a ragged breath and clutched her purse close to her chest. "Yes."

"Well?"

Her eyes widened. "I can't tell you."

"What? That's ridiculous. If you have a problem with someone, tell me and I'll take care of it for you."

Ali's brows knit together. "Why would you do that?"

He stepped forward, propping a hand on the truck above her head. He leaned toward her. She was so close. If he dropped his head, he could kiss her. Taste the sweet lips he'd dreamt about for the eight years he'd been gone. He wanted to, badly. Would she meld against him like she used to, or would she slap him and run?

"Nine years ago, I made a promise to protect you. I went and made a real mess of that, but I'm back. You can call on that promise if you want to. I'll be here for you. You hear me?"

"I'll be fine. I just have to walk to Mahoney and Strong—Tripp's an associate with the law firm. It's not that far." She looked around him toward downtown. Jealousy curled in his chest.

"I can drive you there." He hated himself for being any

part of bringing her near Tripp, but he'd just made a promise, and he'd stay true to it no matter the personal cost.

"I'll walk."

"It's farther than you think, and it's hot as blazes out here. Let me drive you."

She shook her head.

"Can I pick you up from his office and drive you home?"

"I'm sure Tripp will drive me home. I'll see you around."

She brushed past him, but the sweet smell of her lingered—something flowery. Jericho walked back to his Jeep. His pop would have to wait another day or two for a reunion.

He needed to find four new tires and get them on that beastly truck before Tripp could swoop in with some kind of heroic act.

Chapter Four

With his legs tossed over the edge of the porch, Chance swung his feet, banging them against the house with the rhythm of an Indian drumbeat.

Ali leaned an elbow on the armrest of the Adirondack chair, resting her chin on her palm. "Hey, little man, cut that out."

"Is that your truck, Mom?" He sprang to his feet and squinted in the direction of the driveway.

Her green monster of a vehicle rattled over the gravel. "Looks like it. I left my keys with Tripp, and he said he'd have someone fix the tires. That must be him." She pushed up out of the chair and crossed to the steps.

The man climbing out from the driver's side looked about the same size as Tripp, but that's where the similarities ended. Ali pursed her lips.

Chance jostled past her. "Jericho!"

"Hey, bud." He touched the brim of his hat. "Ali."

She narrowed her eyes. "Why do you have my truck?"

He looped his thumbs in his pockets. "You left it at the nursing home. It's got new tires. The old ones couldn't be saved. But these are good ones. You won't have to put chains on them in the winter."

"I'll go inside and get my purse. How much do I owe you?"

"Nothing."

"Nothing? The tires I had were almost bald. I priced out new ones weeks ago, and the lowest I could find from anyone was around a thousand. I can't...won't be able to give you all of that right now, but I can mail you the rest and—"

He shook his head. "Like I said, you don't owe me anything. But your engine's making an unnerving jangling noise, so I'm going to take a peek at that sometime this week."

She thrust out her hand. "My keys."

"Funny thing about that." He leaned a foot on the steps and rested his hands on his knee. "I didn't have keys so I had to hot-wire it." He scratched his neck. "Hadn't done that since high school. Remember how we used to drive Principal Ottman up the wall?"

Ali bit back a grin. "He never could quite figure out how he kept losing his car, or why the police kept finding it at Dairy Queen."

Chance leaped off the last two steps, landing beside Jericho. "What's hot-wire?"

"Well, it's how you can drive a car if you don't have keys. You see, first you take a screwdriver and pull the trim off the steering column. Unbolt the ignition switch, then—"

Ali cleared her throat.

Jericho's lips twitched with the hint of a smirk. "Right. Not something you need to know, bud."

The front door creaked, and Kate popped her head through the opening. "Al? Oh hey, Jericho. Your hot chocolate's boiling over. I shut it off. Hope it's not scalded."

Ali slapped her hand over her heart. "I'd completely forgotten. Do you still want cocoa, Chance?"

Her son's affirmation propelled her into the house. She stuck a spoon into the pan full of liquid chocolate. She brought the hot cocoa to her lips, blowing on it before tasting. "Still good."

Kate set out three mugs. "Jericho can have my cup. I'm headed upstairs anyway."

"He's not staying."

"Guess again, sis. He and Chance are already out there, cozy together on the steps. It sounds like they're swapping tall tales."

The ladle rattled in Ali's hand. "He can't stay. I don't want him on our property, not near Chance."

"Too late." Kate drummed her fingers on the counter. "Did he fix your truck?"

"The tires."

Kate let out a long, low whistle.

"And he won't let me pay him back. Not like I have the money to anyway."

After wishing her sister good-night, Ali hugged the three mugs of steaming cocoa to her chest and strode back outside. Chance popped up, reached for his and then hunkered back down so close that he bumped knees with Jericho. She handed a cup Jericho's way, and his fingers slipped over hers in the exchange. Ali inhaled sharply.

He took a sip, then tipped the mug at her in a salute. "This is good."

She wrapped an arm around her middle and looked out to the Bitterroot Mountain Range. The snowcapped peaks laughed down at the fading sunlight in the valley. The sides were blanketed in a vivid green tapestry of pines. Each canyon crag vied with the peaks for splendor. The Bitterroots calmed her. Taking them in reminded her that even when life felt topsy-turvy, purpose and beauty remained in the world.

"It's from scratch. Mom says none of the packaged stuff in our house, right?" Chance beamed at her, a whipped cream mustache covering his top lip.

"Right."

"Jericho told me he used to ride the broncos in the rodeo.

Isn't that cool? But he said he never rode the bulls. He said it's too dangerous, just like you always say."

Ali leaned her shoulder against a support beam on the porch. "Yes, Jericho used to ride the broncs. He used to rope in the rodeos, too."

Chance plunked down his mug. "Sounds like you were more than neighbors, 'cause I don't know things like that about old Mr. Edgar, and he's lived right across the field my whole life."

Jericho shifted to meet her gaze. He raised his eyebrows.

She let out a long stream of air. "We used to be friends, Chance, that's all."

Chance tapped his chin. "Does that mean you're not friends anymore?"

Jericho kept staring at her. His intensity bored into her soul, and she looked down.

"Jericho's been gone a long time."

She wandered down the steps and into the yard. Their pointer, Drover, trailed after her. She scratched behind his ears, causing his leg to thump against the ground in doggy-bliss.

That had been a close call. Too close. But it's not like she could kick the man out right after that conversation. Doing so would only raise Chance's suspicion.

The low rumble of Jericho's voice carried as he launched into a story detailing an adventure from his days in the army. "We had to go in helicopters, only way to get there. We could hardly see through all the sand swirling around and—"

"So it was like a beach?" Chance peppered Jericho's monologue with a constant stream of questions.

"Naw. Beaches are nice. This was a desert. Hot. It'd be about one hundred twenty degrees, and we'd have to lug around seventy pounds of equipment on our backs without an ocean to cool off in. Ants all over our food. Not too much fun."

Ali coughed. "I think it's about bedtime."

"No way. C'mon, Mom. One more story."

Jericho laid a hand on her son's head. "Don't argue with your mom, bud. Go on up. You'll see me again. Promise."

With a loud groan, Chance shuffled into the house.

A pace away from her, Jericho rose to his feet, his masculine frame outlined by the light flooding from the house.

She crossed her arms. "I can pay you back."

He stepped closer. "I promised to protect you, remember? I made that pact, and I aim to keep it for the rest of my life. You owe me nothing."

She bit her lip.

He tipped his hat. "Sleep tight, Ali." Then he brushed past her and strolled, hands hooked in his pockets, into the hay field back toward his pa's place.

Sweat trickled down Ali's neck as she lugged the last saddle onto its peg in the barn. The triangular posts drilled into the wall were genius. Much better than tipping the saddles on their sides and storing them on the ground like they had been doing. She made a mental note to thank Rider.

Ali placed her hands on her hips as her mind ticked over the accounting books for Big Sky Dreams. She'd never been great at balancing the ledgers, but even Ali could see that money was missing. But how?

Megan Galveen, the other riding instructor for Big Sky Dreams, sashayed through the back door in black designer jeans.

Ali smiled at her. "You're a lifesaver. Thanks for taking care of Salsa when he started misbehaving. I don't know what made the horse so skittish today. I know you've only been here a month, but have I told you how thankful I am for your help?"

Megan pouted her full, over-red lips and closed one eye,

tapping her sunglasses to her chin. "Oh, only about every day. But please, do go on."

Ali laughed. "Well, enjoy your afternoon off. You know you're welcome at Chance's birthday party, right?"

Her coworker flipped her long, glossy black hair. "A party for seven-year-olds isn't really my thing."

"No, I guess not."

Why had Ali even asked her? The woman was more suited in looks to walk down runways than teach handicapped kids about horses.

Ali glanced down at her own mud-caked boots and dirty jeans. She grimaced. Maybe she ought to spend more time on her looks. She ran a hand over her flipped-out, short red hair. Yeah, right. She worked in hay and horse manure all day, and the only kisses bestowed on her came complete with animal cracker crumbs.

Someone cleared their throat, interrupting Ali's train of thought. She looked up to find her head ranch hand, Rider Longley. The man looked like his name—taller than he ought to be and scrawnier than a cornstalk. With his junked-up Levis, scuffed boots, a blue shirt with white buttons and a new brown hat, he looked the part. But he would have been just as comfortable in a cubicle, wearing khakis while programming laptops. He lacked the cowboy snarl in his face, but he made up for his failings with heart and determination.

He looped a rope over his shoulder. "Someone's been out messing with the fences in the heifer field again. I figure it'll take most of the day to round them up off Edgar's property and mend the cuts."

Ali's heart stopped. "What do you mean, messing with the fences?"

Rider adjusted his hat. "I'm not an expert on these sorts of things, but how the slices are, looks to me like someone snipped through our fences with wire cutters. Cows can cause damage, but not clean breaks like I'm finding."

"That's ridiculous." Megan plunked down her suitcase-sized purse and pawed inside until she fished out her lip gloss. "Who would want to mess with Big Sky Dreams?"

"Dunno." He shrugged. "I'm not a detective. Just know what I see."

Pulling off her hat, Ali swiped a hand over her forehead. Now that Rider and Megan were gone, her thoughts swirled. The threatening note, slashed tires, money missing from the Big Sky Dreams account and now the fences—what was she going to do?

"I brought this for you." Kate came beside her, handing over a chilled water bottle.

Ali held the bottle to her neck, then to her cheek. "Feels good. It's really a scorcher out here today. I hope the old air conditioner in the house holds together for Chance's party."

"It'll be fine. If it busts again, those kids won't care."

Ali stepped forward so she stood in the barn entrance. The wind ruffled through the valley, kicking up the smell of the nearby river and drying the sweat from her body.

"How'd lessons go today?"

She unscrewed the bottle cap and took a long swig, catching dribbles on her chin with the back of her hand. Ali loved nothing more than talking about her handicapped horseback-riding program. "Good. Alan's coming along great. The movement's strengthening his core and helping build some muscle tone." It felt good to know that something she'd started made a difference. "Rebecca's parents told me that her test scores have improved since joining the program last month. Can you believe that?"

Kate squeezed her arm. "That's awesome, Al. How about those two?" She jutted her chin toward the sprawling side yard, near the practice corral where Ali usually ran her horse, Denny, through the barrels. Today two boys practiced their cattle roping. Ali gripped the barn wall. Well, if the broad shoulders and popping biceps of Jericho Freed could be classified as a boy. Okay. Man and boy.

Ali let herself breathe for a moment before answering. "I don't know what to think. First he takes care of my truck, then this morning he shows up on the doorstep with a rope in hand, asking for Chance. What was I supposed to say?"

"I think you did the right thing, Al, by letting him spend time with his son."

"But that terrifies me."

"What? Him being here? Or him with Chance?"

"With Chance. Both. I don't know."

"What did he say when you two talked after the firework show?"

Ali crossed her arms, propping her shoulder against the barn. "He said he wants forgiveness. He said he wants to repair our…marriage." A gritty lump formed in her throat as she watched Chance loop the rope over the fake horns and give a loud whoop. He clapped victorious hands with Jericho, whose deep laugh drifted across the yard. A person would have to be blind not to see the resemblance. They had the same eyes, same unruly hair, same slight swagger in their walk, same full-chested laugh. Ali rubbed at her throat.

Kate touched her shoulder. "What are you gonna do?"

"He's a drunk, Kate."

"I haven't smelled beer around him, and I sure haven't seen him staggering around. He might have been at one point, but it doesn't seem like he drinks anymore."

Ali closed her eyes. "If he'd walked out on you like he walked out on me, would you forgive him?"

"We're called to forgive everyone."

"He gets to turn my life into a nightmare. Then with a little 'I'm sorry,' we act like it never happened? Convenient."

Kate placed a hand over hers and Ali looked down, not realizing that her knuckles had become white from her iron grip on the barn door. She let go of the metal and flexed her hand, drawing the blood back into her fingers.

"I don't think forgiveness has to mean forgetting, Al. The consequences of sin will always be there, and I think he's suffered them. Forgiveness means you grant pardon for what happened. It's you saying you won't be bitter and hold those actions against him."

Ali hugged her middle with both arms. "I can't do that. He left. It bothers me that his life's been fine without me, while I had to struggle and scrape and wish each day he'd come back and rescue us." Her voice caught.

"I wouldn't say he got off easy. He's missed seven years of his son's life. Eight years with the woman he loves."

Ali snorted. "Right. He loves me loads."

"And he's back—maybe now's the rescue you waited for."

She shook her head. "I stopped believing in fairy tales a long time ago. There are no white knights, Kate. No one is riding in to save the day. Life is about pressing on when things happen. It's all about who has the most grit, and I think I've proved my worth."

"Maybe that's your problem." Kate's voice took on a sad tone.

Ali jerked back. "My *problem?*"

"You're right; Jericho's not your white knight, but he was never supposed to be. What chance did your husband have of succeeding with those kind of expectations? He can't be the one to rescue you. Not in the way you need. Just like Ma, you're letting hate and bitterness eat away at you, and you think your misery gained you some sort of badge of honor. You think you can punish Jericho for what he did by closing yourself off and holding him at a distance." Kate thrust out her hand. "But look at him. He's free, Al. You're the one still locked up and suffering. And you will be until you offer forgiveness."

Ali shoved the bottle into her sister's hands. "I have work

to do. Thanks for the water." She stomped back into the barn. Twine bit into her hands as she grabbed a bale of hay.

Her sister could go chew on screws. Kate had no idea. She was so young when Dad died, and Ali had stepped into the gap to take Ma's wrath. What did Kate know of suffering and pain and the consequences of sin?

"Nothing." Ali yanked a razor from her pocket and sliced the twine. Pulling the hay into even squares, she placed a bundle in each horse's stall. Drover, playing supervisor, padded along, making sure each horse got their fair share. She caressed the dog's head and smiled when he yawned.

In the moments when Ali looked back at her short-lived marriage objectively, she could see the truth. The judge should have stamped *disaster* in bold red letters on the marriage certificate. In her needy state, did she drive her husband to the bar? In their small apartment, she'd watched the man who was supposed to save her morph into the man he most despised. Had it been her fault?

She swiped away treacherous tears. Infernal hay dust.

I was so afraid that I'd hurt you, Ali. I loved you so much.

Jericho Freed, hurt her? Not possible, not the way he imagined. If she thought the man possessed any tendency toward violence, he wouldn't be alone out there with her son right now.

No. She saw the man she knew. A memory of Jericho taking a beating from his father to protect a runt puppy flashed through her mind. Then one of him at nineteen years old, stepping in between her and Ma, telling her she won't be speaking to his wife *that way* anymore.

Even that last night, with clear eyes, she could see that he left to protect her then, too. In his own way, Jericho always had put her first, but then what kept him from coming home? Didn't he know how much she needed him the past eight years?

Chapter Five

Ten children tromped like a herd of mustangs around the dining room, over the checkered kitchen floor and out the back door as Ali tried to pull the last of the food from the fridge to set out on the table.

"Don't let the door—"

The last child jumped the three steps down into the yard, and the screen door smacked against its hinges, tearing the hole in the screen a few inches wider.

"I'll fix the screen tomorrow." Jericho took the heavy pile of plates from her hands and set them on the counter.

Heat blossomed on her cheeks. He had no right to look that good in a clean pair of jeans and shined boots. His tucked-in, starched red button-down hugged the coiled muscles in his arms.

The sight made her wish she'd taken another minute to give herself a once-over before guests arrived. But the emotional mess Kate had tossed on her that morning made her work slower in the barn. By the time she came back to the house, less than an hour remained until party time. Enough time to shower, but not enough time for makeup or to blow-dry her hair. Jericho probably thought she looked like a wet prairie dog.

She waved her hand, dismissing his comment. "You don't have to fix that screen. It's been like that for months."

"I know I don't have to. But I don't mind. I have to come to tune that clank out of your truck anyway."

Kate stuck her head into the kitchen, a smile on her face as she looked between Jericho and Ali rearranging the table. "Need any more help in here?"

Ali surveyed the room. "I think I've got the food under control. If you want to get one of the games started outside, that would be great."

Kate saluted and meandered out the back door. Satisfied that everything was taken care of, Ali turned, nearly slamming into Jericho. She gasped. She'd almost forgotten he was in the room with her. *Alone.*

His gaze shifted down and up, then down again.

"What are you staring at?" She wiped her hands on a dishcloth and tossed the rag into the sink.

The hint of a roguish smile pulled at his lips. "You're beautiful. I didn't have a picture of you. For eight years I had to rely on my memory. Couldn't do you justice. It's nice to look at you." Ali wanted to accuse him of lying, but his voice wrapped around her, ringing with sincerity.

"Ha." She tucked a damp clump of hair behind her ear, only to have the doggone thing fall forward again. "Then you need to get out more."

Jericho raised a dark eyebrow. "Nope. I don't need to look anywhere else to know that this—" he swept his hand to indicate her "—is my favorite sight."

She harrumphed. "I'm all wet, and I don't have any makeup on. And I'm pretty sure I'm wearing yesterday's socks. Still the prettiest sight?"

He leaned against the counter. "Yes, ma'am." Teasingly, he continued, "But if you want to get good and soaked, I saw a horse trough out front I could dump you in." He moved toward her.

Ali swatted at his hands. With a laugh, she bumped into the garbage can. "Jericho Eli! Don't you dare. I'm too old to get troughed." She dashed behind the table.

"Mom!" Chance burst through the door. "Can I open presents now?" A battalion of kids trailed in his wake.

"Sure, bud. We'll open presents in the front room right now, and then we'll eat."

"Did you make your chocolate cake? The one made with—" he leaned toward her, knowing he wasn't supposed to give away the secret ingredient "—mayonnaise?"

She winked, and her son's gray-blue eyes danced with merriment. As he clomped away, a wave of joy washed over her. Threatening letters, lawsuits and financial woes couldn't touch her today.

But an unwanted husband could.

Jericho took her elbow, turning her to face him.

"I may be asking you to kick me in the teeth, but I need to know." Jericho stopped and looked down at his boots.

Her heart lurched in her chest. The muscles on the side of his jaw popped, and Ali's gut rolled in anticipation of his question. A drunk she could keep secrets from, but a man who proved thoughtful, patient and kind? Everything a father should be?

But—no. He was still the same man who had run off on his wife without looking back, discarded his responsibility to her when it suited him and left his child growing inside of her. The shrapnel in her heart from his departure still chafed, and she wouldn't open Chance up to that world of hurt. Jericho hung around for now, but he could still leave at any moment. A child deserved better than that.

Walking to the sink, she turned her back to him and rinsed off a plate. "I don't really have time right now."

His footsteps moved closer, but she didn't dare turn around. He was so near. Ali's breath caught in her throat. One look into his earnest eyes would unglue her resolve.

He took a breath. "I've been thinking. I did the math… being Chance's birthday today, and him turning seven…"

Her hands gripped the cool metal of the sink.

"It only leaves two options."

"Two?" Her voice came out small.

"Unless he was a preemie. But he wasn't, was he?"

Ali locked her gaze through the window over the sink, to the corral. "No, Chance wasn't a preemie."

She felt him take another step closer. "Then it happened when I was still around."

Spinning, she faced him, arms crossed. "It? *It* happened? I think you better go."

Her emotions reflected in his eyes. The same torment. The longing for everything to be right again.

"Is Chance…is he mine?"

"Chance is *mine*. I asked you to leave." Ali pushed against his chest, and he caught her wrists. She pressed her elbows into him. "Let go of me."

"Let go of her!" Tripp crossed the kitchen in three seconds flat. Jericho dropped the light hold he had of Ali as Tripp sidled up beside her. "I don't think you're welcome here anymore, Jericho."

"That true, Ali? If you want me to leave, I will." His lips formed a grim line.

Tripp slid his arm around her waist.

She nodded. "I can't deal with you right now. I need to take care of all the people here."

Jericho narrowed his eyes, almost like he wanted to say something more, but then he put on his hat and dipped his chin. "Be talking to you later, then."

When he left, Tripp took hold of her hands. "Alison, tell me what's going on."

"You saved me. I almost told him about Chance."

The pressure of his hands increased a bit. Besides Kate, Tripp was the only other person in town who knew for sure that Chance was Jericho's son. "You can't ever do that. You tell him about Chance, and he'll probably sue you for parental rights, or at least want shared custody."

She broke away from him and rubbed her temples. "What am I going to do?"

"You need to divorce him. Make the separation legal. Divorce is your only option." Tripp said it so easily. *Divorce.* The word tasted sour on her tongue. But the lawyer made it sound like going for coffee. His tanned arms showed from the rolled-up sleeves of his oxford, and his blue eyes seemed to take her in, while his wavy brown hair stayed perfectly in place.

She brushed at crumbs on the counter. "I don't see the point."

"I don't see the point of *not* divorcing him."

"I know him. He won't sign any papers."

Tripp shrugged. "It doesn't matter. He abandoned you. Didn't send word for eight years. No court will deny your petition."

An uproar in the front room drew her attention. She glanced at the door separating the kitchen from the rest of the party. "Doesn't a divorce cost a lot of money? You know about our financial situation."

He waved his hand. "I have a friend at the firm who can do the paperwork for you. I'll take care of everything. I'll need your signature, that's all."

She wrung her hands. "I don't know."

Tripp took her shoulders so she faced him. "But what if… what if another man wants to marry you?"

Her gaze snapped to meet his, and she didn't see a trace of mocking in his blues. Like a spooked horse, panic bolted down her spine. Another man? Did that mean…?

The door banged. "Mom! Look at what Jericho gave me. Where is he? I want to show him how I've been practicing." Chance thrust a lasso into her hands.

She slipped away from Tripp and took the thick bound rope, running her thumb over the rough surface. "He had to go home."

"Aw, man. I wanted him to show everyone. He's so cool." Chance started walking back toward his party, then stopped. "He'll be here tomorrow, right?"

"I think so, honey."

"Good. I like him the best out of all your friends."

She hugged her middle as she watched Chance leave the room. What was she going to do about his growing attachment to Jericho? It couldn't continue. For Chance to be safe, and her life to continue without any bumps, Jericho needed to leave town. Soon. Because if he didn't, Jericho was bound to figure out that Chance was his son.

Adrenaline tingled through Jericho's muscles as he walked the short length of the Silvers' hay field toward his father's expansive land—the Bar F Ranch. The pain in his knees throbbed, almost blinding him with intensity, but he limped without stopping to rest. He'd ice them at home.

He'd like to rub that smug look off Tripp's face. How dare the man touch his wife?

Scooping up a rock, he tossed the stone into the deep gully separating their properties and waited, listening for the *ping* of it hitting bottom. His heart felt about as jagged and bottomless.

No wonder she didn't like the sight of him. Ali hadn't cheated on him. Chance *had* to be his son. Not only had he left his teenage wife, he'd left her pregnant and alone.

Why didn't she tell him? He would have stayed. No. That was worse. To stay for the sake of the child when he hadn't been willing to stay for the sake of his wife? Cow manure ranked better than him right about now.

The army chaplain's voice drifted through his mind. *You are not your past errors. You are redeemed.* Jericho had rejoiced in that. He had learned to live in victory, but he wanted his wife's forgiveness, too. What would he have to do to prove to Ali that he could be trusted? Would he ever get through to her?

Husbands, love your wives, just as Christ loved the church and gave himself up for her.

The scripture whizzed through his head and stopped him cold in his tracks. He looked up at the sky as a burning Montana sun began to wrap purple capes over the mountains.

Love her. Keep on loving her.

That much he could do.

Chapter Six

Jericho stared at the clock on the dashboard.

Twenty minutes.

He ran a hand over his beard. He needed a shave. Maybe he should do that first. No. He refocused his eyes on the front doors of the nursing home. It was now or never.

Never sounds good. But he pushed open the Jeep's door and climbed out onto the sun-warmed pavement.

The over-bleached smell of the nursing home assaulted his senses. The hollow clip of his boots on the laminate floor echoed along with the one word ramrodding itself into his head. *Failure. Failure.* Reaching the door bearing a nameplate reading Abram Freed, Jericho froze. He pulled off his battered Stetson and crunched it between his hands. Then he took a step over the threshold.

The sight of Pop tore the breath right out of Jericho's lungs.

Once the poster of an intimidating, weathered cowboy, Abram now just looked…weak. His hair, brushed to the side in a way that Jericho had never seen, had aged to mountain-snowcap-white, but his bushy eyebrows were still charcoal. Like sun-baked, cracked mud, cavernous lines etched the man's face. The once rippled muscles ebbed into sunken patches covered by slack skin.

Jericho waited for his dad to turn and acknowledge him. Or yell at him. Curse him. But he didn't move. What had the doctor told him about Pop? The call came months ago. Stroke. He'd lost the use of his right side. None of it meant anything at the time. But now he saw the effects, and his heart ached with grief for the father he hardly loved. Abram Freed looked like a ship without mooring—lost.

"Hey there, Pops." He hated the vulnerability his voice took on. Like he was ten again, chin to his chest, asking his dad's permission to watch cartoons.

Pop's body tensed, and his head trembled slightly. With a sigh, he raised his left hand off the white sheet by a couple inches. His dad couldn't turn his head. A stabbing, gritty feeling filled Jericho's eyes as he skirted the hospital bed and pulled out the plastic chair near his father's good side. His dad's eyes moved back and forth over Jericho's frame, and the left side of his dad's face pulled up a bit, while the right side remained down in a frown.

A nurse bustled into the room. "Well, now, look at this, Mr. Freed, how nice to have some company. Saw you had a visitor on the log—thought it was that pretty little lady always popping by." She moved toward his father as she spoke.

Pretty little lady? Jericho scanned the room. A fresh vase bursting with purple gerbera daisies sat on the nightstand next to a framed picture of Chance. The photographer had captured the boy's impish smile, crooked on one side and showing more gums than teeth as his blue eyes sparkled. He was holding up a horseshoe in a victorious manner.

Ali?

The nurse poured out a cup of water and set it on the bedside table. "And who are you?"

"I'm his son."

"Mercy me." The nurse leaned down near Pop, speaking loudly. "I bet you're glad to see this young man, ain't you?"

"Ith...Ith."

Unwanted tears gathered at the edge of Jericho's eyes as he watched his father struggling to speak.

Abram smacked his left hand on the bed and closed his eyes. "I dondt know. I dondt know."

Jericho searched the nurse's face. She offered him a sad smile. "That's the only understandable phrase we get. It don't mean anything. He says it no matter what's being talked about. But he can hear just fine. He likes when people come and talk to him. Don't you, Mr. Freed?"

Pop's drooping eyes slid partially open, and his head nodded infinitesimally.

Everything inside Jericho seized up. He clenched his jaw, blinking his eyes a couple times. His last meeting with his father whirled in his head—him screaming at Pop, blaming his father for all that had gone wrong in his life.

Over the last eight years, Jericho had pieced back together his world. He'd returned to Bitterroot Valley for two reasons—to repair his devastated marriage, and to restore his relationship with his father. But how could he do that with a man who couldn't speak? He wanted his father to tell him that he was sorry for the abuse and neglect after Mom died. But that apology would never come. And like it or not, he had to be okay with that.

"Since you're here, will you help me move your pa?"

"What?" Jericho scratched the top of his head. "I guess whatever you want me to do, just say."

"We try to move him every hour or so. Prevent sores. It helps to fight the chance of pneumonia, which is always a possibility." She leaned back to Pop. "But we'd never let that happen, sweet man like you. We take good care of you."

She motioned for Jericho to move his father, and after a moment of hesitation, he lifted Pop's frail body in his arms. The old man fit against his chest. Tiny. Breakable. His father's right side hung limp, whereas the muscles on the left side of his body pulled, straining for dignity. A flood of compassion barreled through Jericho's heart, burying all the anger he'd felt for the man who'd caused him such suffering. Abram Freed could never hurt him again. His dad deserved to be treated with respect, no matter their past.

The nurse indicated a beige wingback chair. Jericho recognized it from his childhood home. With extra care, he set Pop down. As he began to move away, his father touched his hand. Jericho turned, and Abram pointed to a nearby chair.

He looked back toward the nurse as she inched toward the door and raised his eyebrows. She smiled. "It's okay. Just go on and talk to him."

Clearing his throat, Jericho rubbed his hands together, eyes on the floor. He looked back at his father, and the despair swimming in the old man's eyes unglued Jericho's tongue.

So he began to ramble. Told Pop about the past eight years, and went on about still loving Ali. Told stories about the war, and in the midst of it an emotion filtered across his father's face that Jericho had never seen before. Pride.

Swallowing the giant lump in his throat, Jericho leaned forward, and in a voice barely above a whisper said words he hadn't planned. "Pop. I'm sorry I left that night. I didn't just walk out on my wife. I walked out on you, too. We had our bad times between us, but it was never like that when Mom was alive. I understand now why you drank. Losing the woman you love...I get it. I forgive you."

Jericho waited, bracing himself for the backhand to his face or the kick to his side that didn't come. Instead a soft, weathered hand covered his and squeezed. He looked up and his breath caught at the sight of tears slipping from his father's eyes.

"Forgive me?" Jericho whispered.

With his good hand, Pop patted Jericho's cheek, trailing fingers down his chin as if memorizing every inch of his face. His father sighed. He pointed, shaking his finger at the top drawer of the nightstand.

Jericho shifted his chair and set his hand over the handle of the drawer. "Want me to open this?"

"Yeth, yeth." Pop nodded. He opened the drawer and found a single envelope with "Jericho" written on the inside. Could Pop still write? Or had this always been waiting for him?

"You want me to have this?"

His father waved his arm, motioning toward the framed picture of Chance. Jericho scooped the photo up and handed it to him. Pop stroked the picture, tapped the glass then pointed at the envelope bearing Jericho's name.

Jericho gulped. "Should I open this now, or you want me to wait until later?"

Pop tapped his finger on the envelope and then pressed the packet into his son's hands. Jericho nodded and slipped his finger under the lip. Into his hand tumbled a gold watch and a very thin copper-colored key. The tag on the key ring bore the number 139.

"This is Grandpa's watch. You sure you want me to have it?"

"Yeth."

Eyes burning, Jericho slipped the watch onto his wrist. His dad had worn it every day that Jericho could remember. "And what's the story with this key?"

Pop jabbed his finger at the photo of Chance.

"It has to do with Chance?"

"Yeth. Itha. Tha. I dondt know."

Jericho covered his dad's hand and gave it a squeeze. "Don't worry about it, Pop. I'll figure it out."

Denny's rhythmic pounds worked the knots out of Ali's muscles as he galloped across the wide field near the grove of cottonwoods. The trees stood like a gaggle of old women with their heads bent together sharing gossip. Hunching, she avoided the low-growing branches as her buckskin horse carried her.

She sighed. If Ali could have her way, she'd stay on Denny's back and ride off into the horizon like the heroes did in those Old West movies. No stress. No responsibilities.

"You're better than any therapist money can buy. Know that, Denny?" His giant fuzz-covered ears swiveled like a radar to hear her better.

"What are we going to do, huh, bud?" Swinging out of the saddle, she stood beside him, tracing her fingers against the yellow-gold hair covering his withers. He nudged his forehead into her shoulder, and she laughed. "You know I have a carrot in my pocket, don't you?" She pulled out the offering, giggling as his big lips grabbed the food. The warmth of his breath on her fingertips was as comforting as a loving mother's arms.

What would she do about Tripp Phillips's attention toward her? Ali rubbed her temples. She didn't want that. Not with Tripp. Not with any man. Marriage? No, thank you. But she didn't want to lose his friendship, either.

She walked away a few paces, then leaned against the trunk of the largest cottonwood. She slowly let her body slump to the ground. Cocking her knees, she looped her arms on them and looked out across the river as it rippled past. The scene felt familiar, and she instinctively turned and glanced up at the initials Jericho had carved there so many years ago. Funny, the things that could fill her heart with peace. The crudely chipped *JF loves AS* shouldn't cause anything to stir in her, but it did nonetheless.

What was she going to do about that man?

Denny nickered, as if reminding her of her real purpose. "Thanks, bud." She pulled the now crumpled warning letter from her back pocket and smoothed it over her thighs.

If you value what's important to you, you'll stay away from him. You've been warned.

No more threats had arrived. But that morning, Rider had reported that their fence line bore malicious damage. This time it caused one of the heifers to tumble to her death in the gully. Ali couldn't afford to lose any of the stock so carelessly.

It had been alarming enough to find all the horses in the front yard yesterday morning, and she'd wasted hours catching them. One stall left unhitched, she could believe. But ten stalls unlocked and the barn door left wide open? No coincidence, especially since Ali had been the one to lock the barn last night. And, although she wouldn't give fear lease enough to voice it, she thought she'd heard *something* outside the house while she lay in bed.

Nine years ago, I made a promise to protect you.

Startled by Jericho's voice in her mind, she pushed it away and tried to focus on a solution. One he was not a part of. Wasn't his presence the cause of all the problems anyway? The answer was simple—get rid of Jericho. If he left her alone, this magazine-gluing maniac would stop pestering her.

What Jericho had to say didn't matter. It also didn't matter that he'd showed up this morning on the steps with a giant bouquet of her favorite flower—he'd remembered about the daisies. Nor did it matter that, even now, he buried his biceps in grease, putting her truck's engine back together. Nor that Chance's eyes lit up at the sight of the man.

Ali looked at the sky to keep the wetness from trickling out of her eyes.

She shoved the letter again into her pocket and clicked her tongue to call Denny back to her side. Running a hand down his glossy muzzle, she leaned her forehead against his face.

"And it doesn't matter that it still feels like my heart's a hummingbird stuck in my rib cage each time I see him. Or that he really does seem changed. The ranch. Chance and Kate. Protecting them. That's what's most important, right?" Holding his bridle, she stepped away. His gentle eyes, fringed with thick black lashes, surveyed her for one long moment before blinking.

Climbing back into a saddle that felt more like home than

any other place on God's green earth, Ali gave Denny his head. He cantered across the field as if he knew she needed the easy back-and-forth rocking motion to cradle her lost hope one last time.

Jericho Freed needed to leave. For good.

Denny plunged his lips into the trough. "Go easy, big guy. No colic for you."

"Hey, Mom!" Chance showed up at her elbow. He gave Denny's thigh three solid pats.

"Hey there, Chance-man." She ran a hand over her son's hair that stuck up at all angles. "Where's your aunt?"

Chance rolled his eyes and grabbed the edge of the trough. He used it as leverage and swung side to side. "She's making rhubarb jam. Bor-ing. And I told her that, so she banished me from the kitchen."

"Banished you, huh?"

"Yeah, but Jericho said he could use my help, and he showed me how to fix your truck. Then we changed the oil. Good thing I was there to hand him all the tools. Did you know how dirty your engine was, Mom? Major gross-out. Jericho had to use lots of rags just to see stuff." His earnest little expression made Ali bite the inside of her cheeks to keep from smiling at him.

She nodded solemnly. "That sounds serious."

Handing him Denny's lead, Chance fell into step beside her toward the corral. "And then he fixed a bunch of stuff on our truck."

"A bunch?" Ali wrinkled her nose.

"Yes. You're lucky he had so many tools in his car. He said—" Chance dropped his voice to imitate Jericho's "—'We've got to keep your mom safe. Got to fix all these things.'" Chance shrugged. "Then he did."

Great. What was he trying to do, heap coals upon her head? He was supposed to leave, not make her truck purr.

"I know a secret, Mom. Jericho told me."

Ali grabbed her son's shoulder and clamped down. There was only one secret Jericho would have involving Chance. No. He wouldn't—would he? "Secret?" she croaked.

"You have to promise you won't tell him I told."

"I promise. What is it?"

"I told Jericho that I like Samantha."

Ali's heart started beating again. "Oh, honey, you told me that months ago."

"*That's* not the secret."

"What is, then?"

"Jericho said you were pretty."

Ali rolled her eyes. "Secret's out. He told me that, too."

"But then I told him if he thinks that, he should marry you."

"You didn't!"

Chance gave two nods. "He said he liked that marrying part."

She popped a hand on her hip. "And where is Mr. Jericho right now?"

"He had to clean up, so I told him to use the hose out back and not to go in the house because I knew you'd yell at him. Remember when Drover and I played in the puddle and then we went in the kitchen and you were so mad you turned red? I told Jericho about that, and he said he'd better take his chances with the cold hose."

"He did, did he? Hey, can you do me a huge favor and find Rider for me? Let him know I need to talk to him about the fences."

The ranch—and maybe Chance—were in danger. If Jericho wanted to keep them safe, he needed to leave them alone. That thought propelled her forward. Drover trotted beside her, banging into her leg as Ali rounded the back of the house.

Jericho crouched. With the hose pressed between his arm and side, water splashed out in front of him. He rubbed his grease-covered hands together under the stream.

The Silvers' dog, Drover, pounced forward, snapping at the fountain. "Crazy dog. You're going to get all wet." Jericho laughed and backed up, right into someone. He peeked over his shoulder and spotted Ali, her eyes wide as the moon in surprise. Looking all cute and startled.

"Oh. Sorry." He dropped the hose and it sprayed into the air like a geyser, soaking his jeans and shooting at Ali in the process.

He leaned toward the handle attached to the hose and turned off the water. Then took his time standing. He needed to read her face. Was she upset with him for showing up at her house again? Hopefully not. When he turned, he stepped closer. Ali's mouth hung open, and she blinked a couple times.

Jericho couldn't help himself. Using one finger, he tucked a chunk of hair behind her ear. When he grazed her skin she gasped. The sound made a tight fist unwind in his gut. He had to start telling her what was in his heart. Now or never—or risk losing her all over again.

After another step forward, he cupped Ali's elbow. He licked his lips. "I'm so sorry. I've missed so much. Ali, I—"

"Al!" The back screen door smacked the house as Kate rushed down the steps. Jericho tried to think of a kind way to tell Kate to go away, until he saw the tears flowing down her cheeks.

"What's wrong?" Ali grabbed hold of her sister's forearms, and Kate shook her head several times. "It's Ma. Ali, Mom's dead."

Ali's knees wobbled, and Jericho steadied her. He wanted to hug away the pain in her eyes, but for now he'd have to make do with being whatever she needed.

Chapter Seven

The gold letters on the white clapboard sign announcing Riverview Cemetery seemed a mite too cheery for Ali's taste that morning. Like sheep grazing on the peaks, clouds huddled over the mountains. The minister closed the small outdoor ceremony with a prayer. Blinking away the emotions that blurred her vision, Ali wrapped an arm around Kate, who rocked back and forth, the butt of her hand pressed against her mouth.

"It'll be all right." She rubbed small circles across her younger sister's back.

Tripp and Jericho stood on either side like self-appointed sentinels. Chance leaned his head against Ali's stomach, and she used her free hand to trail her fingers over his hair.

The minister moved toward them, hands clasped over his Bible. "I'll pray for your peace. Please don't hesitate to stop by the church if you need anything."

Ali nodded. "Thank you, Pastor."

Rider stepped forward. He lowered his head, touching the brim of his black hat as he passed. Three other ranch hands followed, murmuring their regrets before leaving.

After a moment of silence, Chance spoke up. "Where is she?"

"Who, honey?"

"Grandma."

Ali let go of Kate and knelt the best she could in her black dress and pumps. She traced a hand down her son's expressive face. Jericho knelt down beside her. He looped an arm around her waist.

She took a breath. "Grandma passed away, sweetheart. She's gone. But now she doesn't have to be in a bed anymore and can breathe on her own."

Chance scrunched up his face, tilting his head to the side in a manner that made him look just like Jericho. "But I saw her in that box." He pointed.

At a loss for words, she looked to Jericho.

He gave a slight nod. "That's not really her in there."

Chance pouted.

"Listen, buddy. There is a part of us, the *real* part, that can't be kept in a box like that."

Chance looked at the coffin, then back at Jericho. Ali wrung her hands together. Why hadn't she prepared Chance better?

Jericho rubbed his bent knee, and a flicker of pain crossed his face. "Do you know who Jesus is, Chance?"

A grin creased her son's face. "Oh, does he work at Taco Time?"

Jericho used his hand to cover his smile. "No. That guy's nice, but I'm talking about a different Jesus. The one I'm talking about created those mountains over there." He pointed toward the Bitterroots.

Chance crossed his arms. "But does he make good tacos? Because—"

Jericho dropped a hand on Chance's shoulder. "You hungry? If it's okay with your mom, I'll take you to Taco Time for lunch, and we can talk."

Chance grabbed Jericho's hand and tugged for him to follow. "I think I need to hear about this guy. If there are tacos involved, he sounds kind of cool." Jericho rose with some effort. He looked back over his shoulder at Ali.

Thank you, she mouthed, and tears gathered at the corners of her eyes. He'd make a good father. How could she keep them apart any longer?

Megan appeared next to her. She squeezed Ali's hand. "It was a nice service. I'm so sorry about your mom."

"I just wish we could have done more for her, you know? I feel so bad. All of ten people showed up. Kate and I were the only ones here because of Ma. Everyone else came to support us. It's so sad."

"I remember you saying once, didn't you, that your mom was happiest when your dad was alive?"

"I can't think of a day she's been truly happy since before the day he died."

"Well, look." Megan swept her hand to indicate the headstone—a large one, with the names Buck and Marge Silver engraved across the front. "She's beside him again."

The only place Ma wanted to be.

"Thank you. We haven't known each other long, but I value our friendship. I'm glad you joined the Big Sky team. I don't know what I'd do without you."

"Oh, you know. It was that or assist my dad at the research lab. No, thank you." Megan smiled and started to walk away, then paused. "It does seem odd, though."

With one last look at the grave site, Ali turned and fell into step with Megan. "What seems odd?"

"That Rider came. I sure didn't expect that one. But stranger things have happened."

Ali stopped. "Why would that be weird?"

"But he… I guess it shouldn't matter to me if it doesn't matter to you." Megan shrugged.

Ali crossed her arms. "Just go ahead and spit out whatever you're hinting at."

Megan pursed her lips and raised thinly plucked eyebrows.

"I just thought he hated your family. So it makes me wonder why he would show his face here today."

"That's absurd. What reason does he have to hate us?"

"Could you seriously not know?" Megan narrowed her eyes. "His parents…your dad's company…the accident."

A chill prickled down Ali's spine. "What?"

"The semitruck. It was Rider's parents who were killed in that crash. He and his sisters are the ones who cleaned out all the company's funds in the first lawsuit, and they're the ones who are now coming after you. Don't you do a background check on people?"

"I've never run a check on anyone. I didn't even call his references. What if they're all made up?" Ali's hands shook. "No. I can't believe that. That can't be true. Rider is the sweetest guy." How was she to know? She'd been too young when the accident happened. Mom and the lawyers dealt with everything. Tripp was handling the recent civil suit. She hadn't bothered to ask him the details.

"Listen. My sister works at the bank that handles their settlement account. I know it was the last name Longley. Isn't that Rider's last name?"

You've been warned.

Ali gasped. "Do you think? Could all the stuff that's been happening—the missing money, the fences, the horses turned out, the letter—you *don't* think he's capable of that?"

"He's who I've had pegged all along."

"I had no clue." She balled her fists. "I have to fire him."

Her friend grabbed her hand again as they approached the parking lot. "You can't do that. You need proof. Let's catch him at his own game. If he's lunatic enough to be doing stuff, don't you think he'll be even more dangerous if you make him angry?"

"You're absolutely right. I don't know how he'll react. We have to keep Chance safe." She latched onto Megan's arm. "I need proof. Then I'm calling the cops."

"We'll save your family's ranch yet."

* * *

"Guess what?" Her son's new dress shoes galumphed against the wood floor. "I invited Jericho to stay and have supper with us."

"Chance!"

"I told him about our camping trip too, and he said he used to go camping all the time when he was young. So I told him he had to come with us because you're just a girl and maybe you don't know as much about camping as he does."

"Chance Silver!"

"We're still going camping, aren't we? You said if I got an A in summer school we'd go, and I did, Mom. You promised."

"I know, honey. We're still going camping. Now go upstairs and change out of those clothes. The potpie is almost done." He disappeared up the stairs. "And wash your hands, buster!"

"Camping?" Jericho ran his hands over the top of the couch.

He suddenly felt too close. All the emotions from the past two weeks waged war in Ali's mind. She stepped away from him and straightened a pile of magazines on the coffee table.

"He wanted to go with his Scout group, but each boy had to have a parent along. It was all fathers, and I didn't feel right about it being just me with all those men. So Chance didn't get to go, and he's been bummed ever since." She smoothed her hands down her skirt. "I told him if he did well in summer school I'd take him."

"He had to have summer courses? Is everything okay with him?"

"Yeah. He's decent in school, but it's hard for him to stay focused. Math and science seem more difficult for him to grasp."

Jericho tilted his head. "It was that way for me too when I was about his age."

She looked up. Their gazes locked, and her palms started sweating. *He knows.*

"Listen, I don't have to stay, Ali. You've had a rough day." His low voice tickled down her spine.

"It's okay. We have enough." There was no point sending him away. Chance would be easier to handle tonight with Jericho around. Besides, with the loss of her mother, Jericho's presence lent a comforting feel of days gone by.

The next few hours would give Ali a chance to recoup her defenses, and plot some sort of strategy to confront the doubt bubbling in her head like a whirlpool. All the problems in her life felt like rapidly growing monsters, hungrily slurping all her energy and time.

She turned to go into the kitchen, but stopped with her back to Jericho. "Thank you for talking to him today."

"He's a bright kid. He had a lot of questions." He gave a low chuckle.

Ali grabbed the back of the desk chair near the wall. "I haven't really been on close terms with God."

"You're a good mother. Chance is fortunate to have you."

Ali shook her head and backed toward the kitchen door. "I haven't even thought about all that stuff for a long time. The only thing from the Bible I can remember is some verse that says hope deferred makes the heart sick. I've clung to that phrase this whole time."

"I think there's more to that verse…"

She cut in. "Just…thank you. That's all I'm trying to say."

"You're welcome. And, Ali? You can always come back to God. He's waiting with open arms."

He's free, Al. You're the one still locked up and suffering.

She needed to get away from Jericho. For now, she left him in the front room.

Pushing through the kitchen door, she glanced at Kate then crossed to the oven and pulled out the potpie, satisfied with its golden top. Kate silently pulled out three plates as she began to set the table.

"Four plates. We'll need four settings." Ali dumped the

boiled potatoes into the strainer, shook it and put them back in the pot. She pulled out butter, cream and garlic powder, and yanked open the drawer in search of the masher.

"Jericho?" Kate guessed.

"Yes." Ali swiped the back of her wrist against her forehead. "What am I going to do?"

"About Jericho?"

"I think he...I *know* he suspects about Chance. And I won't—I can't—Chance is my son, and I won't lose him."

"You think Jericho will take him from you if he finds out the truth?"

Ali huffed and tossed up her hands, splattering a glob of mashed potato against the rooster backsplash. "He's a cowboy. Chance is captivated. Jericho can rope and ride and wrestle cattle. He can put an engine back together in one day. Chance thinks he'll be more fun to go camping with than me. How can I compete? I'm not cool. I teach handicapped kids how to ride horses. I make Chance clean his room and scold him for not brushing his teeth."

Kate tapped a handful of forks against her chin. "Sure. Jericho's exciting to a seven-year-old. But it's futile to play a competition game in your head. Chance loves you. You're his mother. I wish you could see—could admit—that Jericho is trustworthy. That cowboy in there isn't here to lord anything over you. Actually, he put all the power in your hands when he asked for your forgiveness."

Ali rinsed off her hands and dried them on the kitchen towel. She brought it to her face and pressed the damp fabric against her eyes. "I don't know if I can. I feel so threatened by him—by what forgiving him could mean to my life and to Chance's."

"You think if you open up that cage of bitterness and resentment you've kept your son and yourself locked in, that Chance will run away? But think, Ali—maybe you aren't meant to live in a cage. None of you are."

But her mother's voice echoed deep in her mind. *If he finds out, he'll take your son. No one will stay. You'll be alone.*

The doorbell rang. Since the girls were in the kitchen busy gabbing, Jericho answered the door. The man waiting on the porch was not a welcome sight.

His lips curled. "Tripp? What are you doing here?"

Tripp looked him up and down. "I could ask you the same thing."

"Seeing as my *wife* lives here, I figure it's my place. Now, the town lawyer on the other hand...what business does he have bothering these women on the day they put their mama to rest?"

"Your wife, huh? We'll see how much longer that lasts." Tripp shoved past him, banging his shoulder on the way into the house. The man was the same height and build as him, but Jericho could trounce the loafer-wearer any day of the week.

He followed on Tripp's heels. "And what's that supposed to mean?"

"Tripp." Ali crossed the room. She rubbed her hands on her flowery apron. The gold flecks in her eyes sparkled as she smiled at their old schoolmate.

Tripp took Ali's hand in both of his. He rubbed his thumb over her knuckles. "I kept thinking about the ordeal you've been through, and I had to come over and make sure you were okay. Is there anything I can do for you, Alison?"

Jericho rolled his eyes. "No, I think we've got it about covered here." Ali tossed him a glare, and he had the strangest urge to stick out his tongue at her.

"We were just sitting down to dinner. Won't you join us?"

The group moved to the kitchen, and Ali asked Chance to pull out another place setting. Tripp slithered right into the spot next to Ali, so Jericho took the spot next to Chance and across from Kate.

Chance swung his feet, banging them against the bottom

rung of the chair. "Yes! I get to sit next to Jericho." After slapping Jericho a high five, he turned to the rest of the table. "Do you know how to start a fire without a match, Tripp?"

Ali dished out potpie.

"Smells good, Ali," Jericho said in an attempt to recapture her attention.

Tripp rubbed his hands together. "I don't know how to do that. But I always have matches on me so I don't need to."

Chance thrust out his fork. "Jericho knows. And he's going to teach me when we go on our camping trip, aren't you?"

"Sure thing, short stack."

"Well." Tripp took a long swig from his glass. "Chance, some of us didn't grow up with all the free time in the world. I grew up in a trailer park. My mom didn't have enough money for me to join the Scouts or to buy fancy camping gear. I may not know rough-and-tumble stuff, but I know about working hard for what I want. I know about scrimping through life, unlike others here who had everything handed to them. Some people have an easy life because their fathers were wealthy ranchers. I may not have all that money, but there are more important things I can teach you about than a simple fire."

Jericho slammed down his cup, and water sloshed onto the table. Kate handed him a wad of napkins. He sopped up the mess.

Ali's gaze ping-ponged from Tripp to Jericho.

Jericho cleared his throat. "The potpie is good."

Chance leaned his chin into his hand. "A fire without matches sounds more fun, though."

"But that knowledge is unnecessary if you always keep matches handy. And I do."

"Eat your peas, Chance," Ali snapped.

Tripp laid down his silverware and patted his mouth with his napkin. "So it's true? You're going camping with Mr. Freed?"

"Mom, too."

"Alison?" Tripp's eyebrows rose.

Her cheeks blossoming, Ali pressed back from the table. "Nothing's been discussed yet. More lemonade, Tripp? You're empty."

Seated at the head of the table, Tripp crossed his arms over his pressed oxford shirt. "I hardly think it's appropriate, this camping business. If you need someone, I can hire a guide. They have those for the tourists. I don't think you need anyone else's help." Tripp looked Jericho in the eye, then reached over and stroked Ali's hand. "I still don't know why you're both so set on going camping in the first place. I wish you wouldn't go."

Jericho's heart pounded like a poked bull. His biceps twitched as he balled his hands.

Ali pressed her hand over her forehead. "Let's not talk about this right now."

"Of course. Whatever you need." Tripp rose from his seat. "I have an appointment this evening anyway." He squeezed Ali's shoulder as he passed. "But we'll talk about this later."

Jericho leveled his best cowboy snarl at Tripp. "Or maybe she'll make up her own mind without your say so."

Tripp ignored him. Waved good-bye to the rest of the family and left out the back door. Jericho caught Ali's gaze across the table, and the worried lines around her eyes made him soften his expression. He sent a wink her way, hoping to take away some of the stress in the room. She didn't need more grief in her life. No, Ali needed to laugh more. If he got his way, Jericho would play a part in bringing more smiles to that beautiful face.

Chapter Eight

A week's worth of tension trickled from Ali as she sat in the living room with her family watching a movie. Kate sat with her legs thrown over the arm of the overstuffed chair, while Ali sat on one end of the couch with Chance's now drooping head against her side. The boy's feet were at the other end of the couch, in Jericho's lap.

She sighed. For as far back as she could remember, Jericho and Tripp had always been like two rams with their horns locked in battle. Good thing she had been able to usher Tripp out of the house after dinner. Not that she didn't like Tripp—she did. He was dependable and successful and gave every indication that he cared about her well-being. And he was kind to Chance. What more could she ask from a friend? But that's not all Tripp Phillips wanted anymore, was it?

Kate made a stretching sound, pulling Ali out of her thoughts. "I'm losing the battle with my eyelids. I need to get to bed."

Ali looked at the clock—it was past ten. "We need to get you up to bed too, Mr. Chance." She turned, and his sleeping body slumped onto her lap. "Chance." She put her hand on his side to give a shake, but a warm, calloused hand covered hers.

"Shhh. Don't wake him. I can carry him up to his bed."

Jericho scooted out from under the boy's feet. With great gentleness, he lifted her son into his arms. Jericho cradled Chance's head against his shoulder. Ali began to rise, but Kate stopped her.

"Stay. I'll show him. I'm going up there anyway."

They tiptoed from the room and padded up the stairs. Ali rubbed her eyes and looked back at the television, where *Peter Pan* was playing. The lost boys bopped across the screen, taunting the pirates in one of the final scenes of the movie. Captain Hook nicked some of the fairy dust and now zipped around in the air after Pan. For a minute it really looked like the red-coated pirate would actually be victorious, but then the tick-tock croc jumped out of the water, the colossal crocodile's jaw slicing through the air as it snapped. Suddenly, Peter trapped Hook just feet above the wide-mouthed lizard, and the lost boys began to chant about him being old and alone.

Ali rubbed her hand against her collarbone because the ache in her chest started up again. She wanted to charge onto her feet and yell at the lost boys. They were cruel. For the first time ever, she *felt* for Hook. She watched his face, the emotions transferring from confidence to despair as he let their words sap his happiness away. Feeling the fairy dust failing, he crossed his arms, bowed his head and plummeted into the croc's waiting mouth. The giant beast swallowed his prize and dove back into the water. The lost boys cheered.

Swiping away a tear, Ali hit the power button and chucked the remote across the room. She strode out the door, down the porch steps and into the yard. Taking two ragged breaths of chilled night air, she looked up at the mountains and clenched her fists.

She thought about her mother's funeral. It burned her. No one in the community had bothered to come, and Ali real-

ized she didn't want to live the same life. She didn't want to
end up alone.

The front door creaked. "Ali? What are you doing out
here?"

Jericho.

She hugged her middle as he crunched toward her over the
gravel driveway. Stepping in front of her, he tipped up her
chin, looking right into her eyes, which were brimming over.

"Is it your ma?"

She shrugged from his touch. "More than that."

"It might help to talk."

"I'll be fine."

"What are you doing tomorrow? Can't you take the day
off? I think you need to get away from everything. The loss of
a parent isn't something you rebound from the next day." His
voice dropped, and his eyes softened. She knew how much
he had struggled with the loss of his own mother.

Ali blew out a stream of air. "I can't take a day off. I have
riding lessons to teach tomorrow, and the 'Dream A Little
Dream' event for Big Sky Dreams to plan, and—"

"Can't someone else teach the lessons?"

She shook her head. "You have to be certified. I'm already
running on fewer volunteers than I need, and Megan took tomorrow off so I have to be there."

"I'm not needed at Pop's place. His staff works like a ma-
chine without me. They're used to running the place. It's
been just them since Pop went in the nursing home. I'll help
you. I'll get here early and saddle all the horses and get them
ready before you wake up."

"I wasn't asking…"

He held up his hand. "I know. But I'm offering. I want to
see you doing what you love. I want to understand why this
organization is so important to you."

She knew she should say no. But she did need the help. And

his desire to know the woman she was now felt like a balm for all the raw spots on her soul. "Guess I'll see you tomorrow."

"Sleep in, Ali."

She'd regret it later.

Rolling the heavy wood out of the way of the barn door, Jericho ushered in the sweet tang of freshly cut alfalfa. He walked to the middle of the indoor arena, surveying the training area, impressed with Ali's work. Stalls lined both sides of the barn, and the dirt floor in between could accommodate a class on horseback. Hay and tack filled most of the stalls on the right side, but on the left side, heads bobbed, ready to start the day. The smell of manure, animal sweat, hay and oats swept him back to his childhood.

Thankfully, each horse had a nameplate on their door that matched a name tag on their saddle. The first one read Salsa. Propping the saddle against his shoulder, he lugged it to the corresponding stall. As he came closer, a horse down the line whinnied and pawed its hooves against the wooden planks of the wall.

"Dumb horse," he mumbled. "Wait your turn."

Jericho ran his hands over Salsa's muscular body. He went through the motions, checking for injuries or signs of sickness before saddling the horse.

His thoughts drifted to Ali.

She loved these fool beasts. Especially her Denny. Jericho remembered the day her dad brought home the flea-bitten buckskin. Abandoned and malnourished, he'd come cheap. When Mr. Silver walked the scrawny horse out of the trailer, Jericho thought the best thing for it would be a bullet between the eyes. The pitiful creature had ribs protruding out of his torso like a row of knives, with deep gashes on his sides, and his spine plates stuck out visible like a stegosaurus. But Ali jumped up and down like Christmas morning, squealing. For a full year she babied that horse back to health. To be honest,

Jericho had been eaten up with jealousy over her attention to that horse. But Ali had been right—persistent love had turned Denny into a winner.

The horse at the end of the row whinnied again. No longer pawing at his stall, he gave a full-out kick to the door. Jericho charged down the aisle.

"Doesn't Ali teach you manners? If you were my—" His words dropped off when he read the name on the stall. He heard an eager nicker then saw the giant strawberry roan. "Chief?"

The horse—*his horse*—snorted and tossed his head as Jericho unlatched the stall door. He stepped in, and Chief shoved his muzzle into Jericho's chest, sniffing loudly. "Hey there, old friend. I would've come to see you sooner if I knew you were here." Chief lowered his head, butting it against Jericho.

"He remembers you."

Jericho jolted. He glanced over his shoulder. Ali stood two paces behind him looking cuter than should be allowed at six in the morning.

Turning back toward the overjoyed horse, he scratched Chief's neck and the beast leaned into his touch, releasing a deep sigh. "I had no idea you kept him."

She shrugged then crossed her arms. "You didn't just abandon me when you left. Chief refused to eat. He started picking fights in the herd where we had them boarded. I couldn't afford the fees anyway, so I came crawling back to Ma. I begged her to let me keep them here. I had to work with him every day to bring him back, but I think it was the therapeutic riding that really saved him. Once he finished the training, he was our big confident guy again."

Looking between the woman he loved and the horse he'd ridden since he was a boy, Jericho felt the weight of his consequences heavy around his neck. His throat went dry. "Thank you for taking care of him when I didn't."

"Are you going to take him back, away from here?"

Jericho patted his old friend. "You said he does the therapy riding?"

"He's one of our best. The kids love him because he's so big."

"Then he stays."

"But he's your horse. You have the right to take him back if you want."

Jericho paused, choosing his words carefully. "When we got hitched, he became yours, too. The whole two-becoming-one thing includes possessions. He's yours. I'm glad he's an asset to your program."

She released a long drag of air. "Oh, good. It's hard to find quality horses with the limited funds we have, and the kids love him. I'd hate to have to replace him."

"Naw. This is where he belongs, right Chief?" Jericho patted the roan's red-and-white speckled withers. "I might want to come ride him every now and then though, if that's fine by you?"

Ali reached up and brushed away the bronze-colored mane from Chief's glistening eyes. "I think that would be just fine."

Jericho worked his thumbs over the back of his neck.

"You'll do fine." Ali squeezed his arm. "You're going to be the side walker. You just keep your hand a couple inches behind Eddy's leg while he's riding." She waved to a girl rolling into the barn on a wheelchair, then continued her instructions. "Just don't touch Eddy and you'll be fine."

Walk. Don't touch. Seemed simple enough.

"Doc. Doc. Doc." The small autistic boy tapped his helmet. His eyes looked spacey as he gazed into the arena.

Ali hovered near the child. "Of course you'll ride Doc, Eddy. And this man here is going to walk beside you, if that's okay? Jericho is new, so you'll have to help him."

Kate led out a roly-poly brown horse with a white blaze down his face. The child's hand shook, and he started chanting the horse's name louder when the animal stepped in line with the mounting stairs. Worrying the horse might act up with all the noise, Jericho transferred his weight onto his better leg, just in case he needed to take quick action.

Did Ali really know what she was doing? An accident with one of these kids could be catastrophic. The children were unpredictable around the animals—and a horse needed strong, confident handling, which Jericho doubted the students would have. Ali said she had some sort of certification that gave her the ability to teach therapeutic riding. But was it safe?

She brushed up beside him and explained in a low voice, "Eddy was nonverbal when he started the program. *Doc* is his first word."

Jericho gaped. "He couldn't talk?"

Rounding the brown horse, Ali helped Eddy climb into the saddle. The small child started clapping. Ali's voice was bathed in patience as she talked to the child. After the two other riders in the lesson mounted their horses, Ali strolled out to the center of the arena. Kate and two other volunteers led the horses around the edge of the circle. Ali pulled out cards for a game, handing a stack to each side walker.

"Ride to the red barrel. Touch your horse's back three times." Jericho read the card out loud.

Kate smiled, looking over her shoulder for instruction from the rider. "Where should we make Doc go, Eddy?"

The boy pointed at the red barrel near the front of the barn.

"Excellent job, Eddy!" Ali called, then turned to offer praise to a student who weaved their horse through the striped poles.

After the lesson was completed, Ali waved goodbye to her students and stayed in the barn talking to parents. Jericho made himself busy, scrubbing out water buckets and putting away tack. When she finished, he ambled over to her.

"What did you think?" She beamed. Jericho's breath whooshed out of his lungs at the sight of her. Ali was incredible.

"I'm glad I came. I think I understand a little more why this means so much to you."

She shrugged. "I fit in here, doing this. I love horses and children, so it works. I'm just glad riding can be used to make someone's life better."

"I can tell they were all having fun, but I guess I don't know enough about the particulars to understand what the riding does for the kids." He looped a lead rope over his hand.

She peered into a horseless stall, checking the tack hanging inside. "Did you know that a horse's gait mimics the human gait? The strides are almost identical. So when the kids are riding, the muscles they need to strengthen are being used without them even realizing it. I've read stories of students who couldn't walk learning how because of the therapeutic riding."

"Sounds pretty cool."

An idea had been nagging him since the beginning of the lesson, and he decided to feel it out. "Is this just something for kids, or would the therapy work for adults with problems, too?"

"Therapeutic riding definitely works for adults with a spectrum of issues."

"What about an amputation?"

"Yes. Therapeutic riding has been shown to speed the acclimation to a prosthetic."

Bingo. His idea took root, and suddenly purpose surged through his veins. Since returning home, his dogged drive had been to win back Ali alone, but he knew he needed to figure out the rest of his life now, too. Would he ranch like his dad? He'd thought before that he'd stay in the army, but that wasn't an option now. But this new plan? It just might work.

Ali moved aside the curtain and peeked out the window as Tripp spoke. He'd come to discuss payment options for the rest of Ma's debt.

"I don't like it, Alison, not one bit. What is he after?"

She snapped up. "I'm not following. Who are you talking about?"

"Freed."

She leaned her head against the glass. "I don't think he's after anything. I think he's just back."

"But he's been here—at your home—every day since he's returned. You don't find that strange?"

Working her lip between her teeth, she scanned the horizon, so sure she had just seen movement. "We were close growing up. Jericho never really had many friends besides me because of how his dad was."

Tripp took hold of her elbow and made her face him. "I think there's more to this that you're not saying. You know better. It makes me sick to stand by and watch history happen again."

"Tripp, I guess I don't know why this concerns you."

He stiffened, like she'd slapped him. "If that's how you feel, I can leave. I just—I considered us good friends, and I'm worried about you."

She laid her hand on his forearm. "Sorry. I didn't mean to sound harsh." She laughed. "*I* don't even know what I think. How can I voice what I don't understand?"

Pushing up his sleeves, he braced both hands on the counter behind him. "I guess the situation nettles me. I mean, this guy brought nothing but trouble into your life. And if that's not enough, then he leaves you and you have to struggle and work sixty-some hours a week just to survive." His voice rose. "Don't deny it. I've watched you ever since we were kids. He's got some sort of magic over you. He's trash, Alison. He's never treated you right, and now you're just running back to him."

Ali clenched her fists. "Jericho Freed is not and never will be *trash*. And I am not running back to him. He's just around."

"Sounds like a lot of heartache if you ask me."

"Then what would you have me do?" She crossed her arms and leaned against the counter opposite him.

Tripp let out a breath and stepped closer, drawing her hands into his. "I would have you choose me instead."

"Choose you?" she whispered.

"Let me draw up the divorce papers."

"But I—"

"I want to marry you, Alison."

A flutter of panic tickled her stomach. Marry Tripp? But Tripp didn't love her.

"Hear me out. I'm trustworthy. I'll never leave you like he did. I will always be here for you. And Chance." He licked his lips. "I want to adopt him after we're wed."

A loud *clang-cla-clang* made them jump.

"Sorry…I…ah…sorry." Megan dropped to the ground, cheeks reddening as she scooped up the empty popcorn bowl. "Kate and I…our movie is finished."

"It's okay, Megan. Tripp was just leaving, and I'm heading to bed." Ali took the metal bowl from her and rinsed it in the sink.

Tripp looked between them like a scolded boy. He inched his way to the back door. "Remember, just say the word, Alison. I can take care of everything."

Even though he was a good friend, Ali was thankful when the door closed behind Tripp. Upstairs in her bedroom, she pressed her fingers to her temples. Marry Tripp? She didn't love him, and certainly didn't appreciate his controlling tone tonight. Then again, love had gotten her into trouble in the past.

Chapter Nine

"Well, all your paperwork looks to be in order, Mr. Freed. We just need to run some numbers, and I'll let you know what else you need to do to get this corporation off the ground. It doesn't look like there'll be any problems."

"Thanks." Jericho fought the itch in his fingers to yank a gap in his tie. The fool contraption always choked like a tightened noose. He ran his palms against the stiff fabric of his dress pants. While the bank employee typed at the desk, he picked up her nameplate, and it fumbled to the floor. He lunged to pick it up, smacking his head on the edge of the desk on the way up.

The young loan officer hopped to her feet. "Oh, dear, are you all right, sir?"

Rubbing the back of his head, he smiled. "I'm fine. Smarts my pride the most." He read the nameplate before setting it back on her desk. "Miss Galveen." Jericho scrunched up his brow. "Why does your name sound familiar? Did you grow up around here?"

She blushed. *Oh, just great.* She thought he was feeding her a pickup line.

"No. We're new in the area. Maybe you know my father?

He works at the Mountaintop Research Laboratory." Pride laced her voice, and her chin went up a notch.

Jericho rubbed his freshly shaved chin. "Aren't they helping with research for bioterrorism? They work with some pretty dangerous chemicals, from what I hear."

She nodded. "Oh, yes. Everything they do there is very top secret."

"Impressive, but I don't rub shoulders with the doctor types there, so I don't know why your last name would stick out."

She pushed up her glasses. Then resumed tapping on her keyboard. "I have a sister who lives around here, too. Megan? She works on this Podunk farm near the outskirts of town."

"It's actually a ranch. Not a farm. I know the owner pretty well."

She straightened the bracelets on her wrists. "Small world."

"Does it look like everything will work out? There's a lot of paperwork involved, and I want to get this rolling as soon as possible."

"For now, things look great. But you do know, with this kind of undertaking, you're going to need a lot more capital. Do you understand how much money this will take to run? That's even if you can get it off the ground. That alone will take a significantly bigger sum than this loan. I'd hate to see you under water before your business has a fair chance."

"Don't worry. I have money coming to me."

She stopped typing and quirked an eyebrow. "Coming to you? How intriguing, Mr. Freed. Well then, if that's the case, I believe you'll be able to start this project soon."

"That's good news." He hooked his ankle on his knee, set it back on the floor then crossed his legs again.

"And might I say, this is a worthwhile endeavor. Even without the capital, I think there would be many individuals and organizations willing to donate to something like this."

Jericho nodded. He didn't need their money, but it was good to know the community would be behind him.

* * *

"More chicken salad, please." Chance shuffled over, plate in hand.

"There's plenty here." Ali dished another serving onto one of the sweet rolls she'd baked that morning and handed him the sandwich. The branches of the cottonwood trees swayed above them as the river gurgled a calming tune. Chance squished against her side, and she slipped her arm around his shoulder. She dropped a kiss to the crown of his head while he munched.

"We should do this every day. I love our picnics."

"I do too, bud." Ali pulled a caramel brownie from the basket. "We have to eat these before they get too gooey to handle."

Chance popped to his feet. "Hey, someone's coming."

Ali spun around. "That's Chief."

"It's not just Chief. Someone is riding him."

"I see that, Chance." She squinted, then sucked in a ragged breath. "It's Jericho."

Chance charged into the clearing. Hopping, he waved like a distress signal. Jericho swung down from the giant strawberry roan and gave Chance's shoulder a squeeze before tipping his hat to Ali.

She slunk against the tree and drew her knees to her chest. Why was he here? Did he remember it was their anniversary? Of course not. He never cared about keeping track of dates. He forgot her birthday that year they'd been married.

"Hey, pal, can you help me find a place to tie up Chief?" His voice awakened a flock of butterflies in her stomach.

"You don't have to tie him up. Mom says Chief is better behaved than me sometimes. Isn't that right, Mom?" Chance bobbed forward, his hand clasped in Jericho's.

"That's right, Chance." She gave Jericho a stiff chin-up greeting. "If you loop his reins over the saddle horn, Chief will hang out near that clover patch. He's been trained not to wander off."

Jericho cleared his throat. "Good to know. You've worked wonders with him. I don't remember Chief being so well behaved."

Ali hugged her legs tighter. "Yeah, well, men like to take off."

The blanket shifted as Jericho sat down. "Then that means Chief's a testament that a man can learn to stay put."

She uncoiled her body and ran her fingers against the stiff seams of the basket. "He's a horse." She took a deep breath. "What are you doing here?"

"Kate told me you guys were out here."

"'Course she did."

His work-worn hand covered hers, and he dropped his voice to a whisper. "Do you want me to leave?"

Chance grabbed Jericho's hat and plopped it onto his own head. "We're having a picnic, because today is our special day."

Heat raced up Ali's neck. She jerked her hand from under Jericho's.

He raised a dark eyebrow. "Is it now? Do you want to hear the strangest thing in the world?"

Chance's eyes widened, and he nodded vigorously.

"Today's my special day, too." He tapped Chance's nose.

Ali's gaze locked with Jericho's. His eyes softened. A wave of warmth rushed through her heart. *He knows. He remembered.* A string of goose bumps raced up her arms, but just as quickly they vanished. Kate must have told him. Meddling sister.

Chance dropped to his knees. "Well, if it's your special day, then you should share our picnic."

Jericho kept staring at her. "What do you have there, bud?"

A crunching sound announced Chance's effort to paw through the basket. "Chicken salad and pasta salad, but don't worry. Just because they have 'salad' in their names doesn't mean they have lettuce. I hate lettuce. And Mom says with all the mayo, they're not even good for you. We have brownies, but they're getting mushy. Maybe you should eat one of them first."

Ali looked down, breaking the spell Jericho had over her. She swiped away auburn hair from her face and grabbed the basket when Chance pilfered a second brownie. "We only brought out two sets of plates and silverware. I hope you don't mind using dirty ones." She made Jericho two sandwiches, scooping a generous helping of pasta salad on the plate before handing him her utensils.

Chance giggled around the brownie bits in his mouth. "Gross. You're going to get my mom's girl cooties."

With a wink that sent Ali's heart galloping, Jericho smirked. "I'm not too worried about sharing any of your mom's cooties."

Jericho lifted the basket and blanket from Ali's arms when they walked back toward the ranch house. Chance bounded between them, clutching Chief's reins in his hand. Jericho glanced over to Ali, but her gaze darted away. Discovering that she still celebrated their anniversary had given him cause to hope.

"What do you two have going on the rest of the day?"

"I have to go to Walmart with Aunt Kate." Chance shuffled his feet.

Ali sighed. "There are three classes to teach this afternoon. It's going to be a long day."

Jericho switched the basket to his other hand. "I can stick around and help if you need more volunteers."

Ali ran her hand over Chance's head as they neared the house. "Can you put Chief in his stall for me so he's ready for Brandon to ride?"

She started up the stairs to the house, then turned to take

the blanket from Jericho. "I don't know if it's the best idea for you to stick around."

"Are you still down volunteers?"

"Well, yes."

"Then why not? I sure hope you don't say I failed last time, because I thought my side-walking skills were legendary." He tried to wink at her, but she turned and grabbed the railing.

Standing near the front door, she pressed her thumb and forefinger against her eyes. "Do you even know what day it is? How difficult this is?"

She whirled to walk into the house, but he captured her arm and made her face him. Setting down the basket, he placed his hands on her shoulders. "Today is the nine-year anniversary of the day the girl of my dreams married me. It was the happiest day of my life. I could never forget."

Tears made her eyes look like melted chocolate. His gut twisted. He never wanted to be the cause of this woman's tears ever again.

She pushed up on his wrists. "You only know that because Kate reminded you."

"Your anniversary gift is in there on the table."

"My gift?"

"I owe you a heap more. I'll make up for the lost years too, if you'll let me."

Her eyes widened. "You got me a gift?"

"Don't get too excited. It's not much. Go on in there. I know how you can't wait to tear off the paper. Remember that Christmas when you found your presents early?" He chuckled at the memory of finding her in their front room with scraps of paper all over.

"I warned you that if I found them, they were fair game to open." She pushed through the front door and beelined for the gift. She lifted the item in her hands before meeting his gaze.

"Go on. Open it." He smiled.

She tore off the ribbons and shredded through the paper.

Jericho laughed. Good thing he'd convinced the lady at the store to wrap it for him. Left to him, the thing would have been tossed in a bag and handed to Ali.

She pried open the box and peeked inside. Her gasp caused warmth to spread through his chest. She pulled out the horse statue and examined the sculpture from every angle. "Jericho, this is beautiful."

He crossed the room and took a seat beside her on the couch. "I'm glad you like it."

She traced a finger over each of the three horses carved in stone. Her favorite beasts were captured in a steady sprint together, hair flying. Free. "What is it made out of? I've never seen anything like it. Not this shade of red or with bands in these colors. It's so unique."

"It's made from a block of Jasper. I saw it and knew I had to get it for you." He'd searched for the perfect token for weeks. A diamond ring had been his first thought. As young as they were when they got married, he never gave her an engagement ring or wedding band. But Ali wouldn't have accepted anything like that. Not yet.

She set the statue down and moved back, surveying it.

Jericho picked it back up and turned toward her. "See, I chose it because there are three horses. I figured they could be like you, me, and God. That's what was wrong before. We left him out completely. But we can be like these horses. We can gallop together."

He only wished there had been one with a smaller fourth horse so he could let Ali know that he wanted Chance, too. Staring at the statue again, Ali fanned her face, making Jericho smile. Just maybe they'd become a family after all.

Ali performed rapid-fire blinks to keep the moisture from leaving her eyes. Jericho Freed sat inches away, going on about dreaming together as she fought an urge to toss her arms around his neck and beg him to come back and truly be her husband. She watched his lips move over the words. Did his kisses still have the power to set her brain spinning? She leaned a little closer.

The front door jerked open. Megan appeared. "Are you doing lessons today?"

Bolting up, Ali looked at the clock. "I'm sorry. I didn't realize—yes, I'll follow you out." She skirted the couch. Jericho rose and followed her through the front door.

Ali forced herself to breathe. She needed to be careful. She didn't know if she could handle any more time with Jericho without doing something she'd regret later.

Chapter Ten

"Can't I go to Mark's house? Puh-leaze, Mom?" Chance walked beside her, the shiny pail smacking against his calf with every step.

Ali racked her brain, trying to remember which one of the kids was Mark. The one whose parents let them ride the ATVs? Definitely not happening.

"No, pal, I need you to help me." Straightening her glove, she swiped the back of her wrist against her forehead.

"This is the worst day ever. Mark's parents don't make him scoop poop." He slammed the bucket on the ground of the training corral, releasing a puff of dust into the air. She coughed into her elbow then raked up manure, tipping it into the pail.

"Well, I'm afraid Mark won't know a thing about running a ranch when his parents leave it to him, but you, sir, you'll be able to do everything."

"Maybe I don't want to work on a ranch." Chance stomped his boot, his eyebrows drawn.

Grabbing the handle, she pushed the bucket back at him. Her hands shook. Didn't want to work on a ranch? "You can't mean that. All this property will be yours one day."

"I don't want it. I want to move far away and never scoop poop again."

"Who will take care of the horses and the cattle if you don't?"

"This stinks," he mumbled.

"Watch your attitude, mister."

With eyes blazing thunder, Chance dropped the bucket again. "If I had a dad, he'd be here helping us, and we wouldn't have to work so hard all the time."

"Well, it's just us so—"

"Where is my dad, huh? Why don't you talk about him?"

Ali bit down on her lip. She reached for her son, but he yanked away. "Honey, we've talked about this a million times. You know the story."

"No. Not really. You only told me you were too young and that my dad had to go. I heard you tell Aunt Kate that you should have never married him, that it was one big accident." Chance trembled. Ali tried to reach for him again, but he shoved against her with so much force that she winced.

"My relationship with your father was a mistake, but *you* are not. Do you understand me, Chance? You're the most important person to me in the whole world."

"Everyone else has a dad. Why can't I? Didn't he want me? Is that why he's gone?" He swiped at hot, angry tears.

Everything in Ali ached to take him in her arms, to kiss away the hurt and rejection revealed in the bent of his brow, but for once, she didn't know how to cool his temper. This was exactly why Jericho couldn't be told. Look what perceived rejection did to her son. If Jericho walked away from Chance after they both knew, the destruction would be irreversible.

"Chance." She knelt down in front of him, the dry earth coating her jeans. "Your dad left because he didn't want *me*." The words sliced as they came out. "He didn't even know about you, sweetheart."

"Then maybe you should tell him. It's not fair. He might

not want you, but what if he wants me?" He spat out the words.

His little fists shook. Thin as a reed in the wind, his chest heaved. "Why do Jericho and me have the same eyes, huh?"

Bile crept up the back of Ali's throat. "Blue eyes? A lot of people have blue eyes."

"Not like these." He jammed a finger toward the offending body part. "Our eyes are the same color as the slushies from the gas station. The electric blue ones."

"Cha-ance." She dragged out his name. "A lot of people have blue eyes. Tripp has blue eyes like yours, too. It doesn't mean anything special."

"But how come Jericho and I laugh the same?"

"You're not making any sense, honey. Now grab that bucket, and let's do the other side of the corral."

With a growl, Chance kicked the metal bucket, sending manure into the air. Ali rocked back, throwing her arms over her head to block the raining mess.

"Chance Silver! Get to your room this instant."

He started to stalk off, then whirled around. "Know what? I'm going to find my dad. He'll be nicer than you, and he won't lie to me like you do." With that declaration, he charged off toward the house.

Ali tried to stand, but her knees wobbled. The handle of the metal bucket shuddered in her hand.

It started already. She was losing her son, and she didn't know how to get him back. She slumped to the ground. Her hands dropped into her lap, and she just stared at them, numb with swollen emotions.

Head in her hands, Ali didn't look up from the kitchen table when the back door creaked open, followed by the telltale slap of the screen door against the house.

"Hey, I was looking for you. I want to talk… Are you okay?" Kate dropped into the chair beside her.

Ali sighed.

Kate ran her hand across the tabletop. "Huh. How's that for bad timing?"

Ali leaned her cheek on her hands. "Bad timing?" She lifted her eyebrows.

"I was looking for you everywhere. Couldn't find you or Chance."

"Chance is in his bedroom. I'm considering keeping him locked up there until his eighteenth birthday. What do you think?"

Kate's eyes widened. "Don't tell me you caught him yanking feathers out of the chickens again?"

Ali offered a slight smile. "Worse. He wants to know who his father is."

Kate whistled, long and low.

"That about says it."

Pushing up from the table, Kate crossed the room to the fridge. "Well? Are you going to tell him?"

"I can't. Chance doesn't even know who his father is, and he already likes him more. Think if he found out for sure that it was Jericho."

Popping open a take-out container, Kate gave it a sniff and pulled a face. "Do you seriously think Chance isn't smart enough to find out? I mean, he might not figure it out today, but if Jericho is going to stay in Bitterroot Valley, and if he keeps hanging around here, Chance is bound to put it together."

Ali grabbed the edge of the table with wrought-iron strength. "He asked why they have the same eyes."

Dumping three offending containers from the fridge into the trash can, Kate shrugged. "I honestly don't see why you keep lying to both of them."

"I'm not lying." Ali ran a hand through her hair. She didn't like being called a liar twice in one day. "I'm just not telling them. That's not the same."

Kate rolled her eyes. "Whatever. If it makes you feel better to believe that, then you're lying to more than just them."

Ali rose. "Where do you get off, Kate? Seriously. You can't stand there and judge me. I'm sick of it. I'm sick of not living up to anyone's expectations. I'm sick of you and your perfect little life and you spitting out platitudes."

Kate jammed down the garbage lid. "Sick of it, huh?"

Boiling over with emotions that had nothing to do with her sister, Ali thrust her hand. "Makes me want to puke."

Kate leveled a glare. "Good. That makes my news easier to tell you. I found a job. I'm leaving."

"Leaving?" Ali stumbled back and blinked. "But why?"

Kate tossed up her hands. "This isn't where I belong, Al. It's never been my world. You live and breathe these animals, this land. I don't. At all. I don't like working with the horses. I don't like doing manual labor in the heat. I don't like being able to see for miles and miles. The bugs. None of it."

"I don't understand."

"Ali, think about it. Unless you're too blind to see, your prodigal husband has returned. I've lived my life helping you long enough, and you don't need me anymore. Move on, sis. Forgive your husband and live a new life with your family."

Ali swallowed a lump the size of Montana. "Is that how you really feel? Like I've held you back?"

"Not in the terrible way you're imagining. But I took off more than a year before starting college to stay with you and help take care of Chance. I stuck close to home for school and came back right away, all so I could be here for you and Ma."

"I never asked that of you. You could have done anything you wanted. Don't blame me for—"

"I'm not blaming you for anything. It's just how it went. I don't regret staying behind with you. But now that I know Jericho is back, I'm going to move on. Finally do my own thing."

Ali searched her little sister's face, trying to grasp what she was saying. "You're really leaving?"

"Yeah. Sorry to tell you like this." Kate walked toward the back door. "But I found a job. I went to college for a reason. Better use that degree, right?" She opened the door and offered Ali a small, soft smile. Then she walked outside.

"Right." Ali stared at the door as it slammed shut.

Pink light, the blush of the first kiss of sunlight, flooded the valley. Ali drank in a fortifying breath drenched with the sweet scent of wildflowers. She pulled herself off the dew-drenched ground and shook the clinging grass from the back of her shirt. Guess she ended up falling asleep out here last night. She stretched against a kink in her neck.

Arms draped around her knees, she relished a peaceful moment spent laughing at the prairie dogs popping in and out of their earthen holes. It made her forget for a short while about all the responsibility weighing her down.

She took a deep breath. "I don't know what You're doing, God, but something is happening and I'm not sure I like it. But at least I can say thank You for new starts."

First there was Chance's outburst yesterday, cured by two hours in his room. He emerged contrite and happy to trail Kate the rest of the day. All talk of fathers abandoned.

Ali still felt uneasy about her ranch hand, though. He didn't strike her as a person who was capable of harming anyone. Was Megan right? Could Rider Longley really be out to get her? Why would Rider give two bucks about seeing her and Jericho together at the picnic? The thought almost made her laugh.

Then Kate's big announcement. *Leaving.* She didn't know how to function without her sister around. Sure, she could be happy for her little sister, going out and making something of herself in the world. It's just that Ali had always counted on the fact that Kate would be *here.*

And what about poor Tripp? Ali wrung her hands. The

man was everything she should want, but couldn't force her heart to love. His attention brought added stress.

Everyone chipped at pieces of her heart then walked away. Ali shivered and hugged her torso. She might be left with nothing.

"Miss Ali!"

She looked up. Across the field, Rider jogged toward her, his mouth in a grim line. Ali rocketed to her feet.

He reached her seconds later, holding his side, puffing out breaths. "Miss Ali, I've been looking for you everywhere. Megan said to get you quick. It's Denny."

Chapter Eleven

Ali tore across the field on the toes of her boots. Her hat flew off. Grabbing the door of the barn, she used it to bank hard and round down the aisle. A couple horses snorted when she entered. Denny's stall stood open.

Megan sprang to her feet. "I don't know what's wrong with him. He won't get up and—"

Ali pushed past her. Denny lay on his side, eyes closed. His head rested in filthy straw. Dropping to her knees, Ali crawled to him. "Denny? Hey, boy. What's wrong, handsome?"

He didn't stir. Didn't open his eyes.

"How long has he been like this?" She groped her hands over his body, searching for an injury, hoping he'd nicker or snort. He felt warm. Much too warm. And he heaved more than breathed, as if he couldn't fill his lungs.

Megan stepped back. "I don't know. I found him this way."

Trembling, Ali looked over her shoulder to Megan, who propped her shoulder against the doorway. "How long until the vet's here?"

"I didn't call him yet."

"Do it now," Ali pleaded. Why hadn't she come out to the barn when she'd woken up instead of going out to the field?

She should have known he needed her, should have *felt* it. If something happened to him…if he… She shook her head.

Turning back to Denny, Ali ran her hands along his neck, pressing her ear against his side. His heart raced, and her eyes burned. "C'mon, buddy. Stay here with me."

Ali got up and stepped to his other side. Blood pooled from his lips, and her vision went blurry. Kneeling near his head, she pressed her face against him. She drank in the smell of his skin, memorized the play of hay dust against his strong black muzzle.

"I love you. Please don't leave me," she whispered. Her lips brushed his jaw.

He made a weird noise deep in his throat, like he was trying to talk to her and couldn't. Ali pulled back. Denny opened the gentle, expressive eye she loved, and his gaze locked with hers for a long moment. Ali held her breath. Her old friend gave one long sigh and closed his eyes again. Black lashes splayed out against his golden fur.

And just like that, he was gone.

No! The word rocked through her, and she wanted to hurl something. She grabbed at the side of the stall, but the moment she found her feet, she turned and looked down at Denny. Her beautiful friend, with his magnificent buckskin glossy hide and his perfect black stockings. She covered her mouth with her hand, holding back a sob as it shuddered, trying to get out of her body.

Gone.

Her knees buckled, and she came down hard beside him. Crawling over his middle, she ran her hands through his mane, cupped them over the soft hairs on the edge of his ears. His body was still warm, possessing the power to make her feel whole. What would she do without him? Riding Denny was the only thing that had ever made her forget the ache inside.

"Denny. I'm so sorry." Her tears exploded one after another on his neck. She moved to lie against his back. A deep moan escaped her lips, and the sobs came then. She wrapped an arm over the top of him and pulled herself closer, weeping.

Kate stepped toward her. "Al. Hey. Let's get you out of here."

Ali lifted her head and shook it. Choking on her emotions, she sat and pushed her sister away. Then she leaned back over her beloved horse, running her hands across the length of his body. She stroked her fingertips down his face.

"After Jericho left, I used to have trouble sleeping. I'd come in here and crawl up on Den. I'd sob into his back and whisper 'come home' over and over again. Denny would breathe even and steady, as if to tell me no matter what—no matter who left—he would always be there for me. I used to come out here and just hug his neck for hours when Ma got bad. And he'd let me, just loop his head over my shoulder and rub his muzzle on my back like he was saying that he loved me, even if no one else did."

"Come on, it's not good for you to stay with him like this." Kate beckoned to her.

Ali curled back down against Denny's back. "Leave me alone."

"Al…"

"I mean it. Just leave me alone with him. Please."

Kate backed out of the stall, motioning for the others to leave the barn.

Feeling like her insides had been ripped out, Ali sobbed into Denny's lifeless body. "I'm so sorry I wasn't here for you. I'm so sorry, Denny."

The Jeep churned the gravel, kicking up a cloud of dust as Jericho pulled onto the Silvers' property. He was late for the riding lessons, but there were no cars, none of the usual bustle. He parked the vehicle, got out and strode toward the barn.

Rider skirted around the side. "Wouldn't go in there if I was you."

"Where is everyone?"

Rider's gaze shifted to the door. "Classes were canceled today."

Ali didn't cancel classes for anything. Jericho grabbed Rider's arm. "What's going on?"

"It's Denny. Ali's in there with him. She won't come out, and won't let any of us in."

Jericho saw it in Rider's eyes. Her horse was dead. *Oh, Ali.*

Pushing the ranch hand aside, Jericho raced into the dark barn. In the commotion, the lights must have never been turned on, and he wasn't about to now and risk startling Ali. He walked into the fifth stall and froze, the air catching in his chest. She lay with her arms around the horse she loved, whispering into his unhearing ears.

Tears stung Jericho's eyes as he knelt, running his hand over her red hair. Ali blinked up at him, and for a moment, he thought she would shove him away. Yell at him to leave. Instead, she sat up inch by inch and cupped her hands over her face. Thinking she was ready to leave Denny's side, Jericho took her elbows and drew Ali to her feet. She let out a loud, mournful whimper that made his insides run cold. He pulled her against his chest, but she crumpled. He went down to the ground with her, holding her while she shook.

"He's gone. He left me." One of her hands shot out, and she stroked the animal's now-cold leg. Jericho took both her hands and ushered her beside him as he sat, leaning against the wall of the stall. He wrapped her in his arms, trying to offer his warmth and his strength. She turned into him, grabbing fistfuls of his shirt as she cried, "Why does everyone leave me?"

"I'm here, Ali. Shhh." Jericho stroked her hair and rubbed circles on her back. He dropped a kiss against her hair. "I gotcha." Blazes of pain raced up his knee, but he wasn't about to risk shifting his weight. Absolutely nothing short of the barn catching on fire would convince him to do something that might force Ali to move. Pulling her closer, he nosed into her hair, smelling the trace of something flowery like the outdoors. *Smells like the sunshine.*

All too soon, Ali put her hand to his chest and pushed a little. She sat back, eyelashes damp, nose blotchy, and eyes red-rimmed.

He'd never seen someone more beautiful.

He wanted to kiss the tears from her cheeks. Instead, he settled for wiping them with the side of his finger. "I'm sorry about Denny. I know what he meant to you."

Uh-oh. That got the floodgates started again.

The next breath she sucked down rattled on the way in. "He was *everything.* I don't know what I'm going to do without him. It hurts. Right here." She laid both of her hands over her heart. "Could I be having a heart attack?"

Pulling up his knee, Jericho finally found a moderate amount of relief. "I think it's heartache, sweetie, not a heart attack."

"It's too much. Why is so much happening at once?" Using the back of her wrist to wipe her nose, she closed her eyes.

He took a deep breath. What comfort could he offer? Her beloved horse lay dead as a stone inches away. No, he wouldn't make light of the loss by trying to tie it up with pretty words, even if he could find something eloquent to say.

When she opened her eyes, her gaze locked with his. The gold specks in her eyes sparkled, and he couldn't breathe for a second. He broke the trance, more out of necessity than anything. He would *not* kiss this woman next to Denny's body.

He cupped her shoulders. "What's too much?"

"Ma just passed away. Now this. You showed back up, and Tripp is stressing me out. Chance is angry with me, and Kate is leaving." Using her fingers, she ticked off the offenses. "The ranch isn't turning a profit, and I'm afraid Big Sky Dreams might not be able to meet our fundraising goals, and then I'm so scared…"

Concern prickled down his skin. "Scared about what?"

Her mouth opened in an O. "Just all this. Everything that's going on."

He could see it. She still didn't trust him. Fine. He could live with that for now. At least she wasn't so bent on pushing him away anymore.

"Don't know how I feel about making it on your list."

"You can't deny that your presence is adding a lot of stress."

"It doesn't have to."

"Jericho, what am I going to do without Denny? I had this big plan. He was going to save us. I had us signed up for six rodeos this summer." She fingered Denny's ear. "I know it sounds stupid, but I had it all planned. We were going to take first place at all six races and use the prize money to pay off the debt and help keep the doors to Big Sky Dreams open. And now?" She shrugged. "Now that hope is gone, and I don't know what I'm going to do."

His heart wrenching at seeing her beside Denny, Jericho scooched over and placed his hand atop hers where it lay on the horse's neck. "Maybe," he whispered. "Maybe you need to look to a different savior."

Her eyebrows rose. "You?"

Shaking his head, he gave her hand a squeeze. "No. I want to help you, if you'll let me. I'd love to be beside you for all that stuff you just said, and do my share of fixing. But I'm no hero to put all your trust in. I'm talking about God."

She snorted. "Now you're starting to sound like Kate. She keeps leaving these three-by-five cards all over the house with verses scribbled on them. Supposedly it's so she can memorize them, but I think she's trying to leave hints for me."

Jericho smiled. "Like spiritual bread crumbs? I knew I liked that girl." Just then, Ali's redheaded sister tiptoed into the barn and Jericho caught her eye, giving her a nod.

"Hey, Al, you okay?" Kate's voice came low as she ducked her head into the stall.

"I don't think I'll be okay for a long time."

"Well, we called the vet and he's making arrangements to have Denny picked up. I don't think you should be here when they do it."

Neither did Jericho. Growing up on a ranch, he had seen his share of dead animals. Often, Pop moved the carcass to the edge of the property and let the mountain lions, bears and wolves have at it, but the few he'd seen hauled away, well, he didn't want Ali to witness it with her beloved pet. The companies were respectful, but seeing them wrap chains around Denny's body and drag him into the truck? No, thank you.

He stood, offering a hand to her. She surprised him again by taking it.

Her lip trembled. "I want an autopsy. Tell Dr. Hammond... I have to know what caused this."

Kate's brow wrinkled. "Al, that's expensive."

Wrapping his arm around Ali's waist, Jericho ushered her out of the stall and slowly down the barn aisle. "I'll pay for it."

Sure that she was going to argue, he racked his brain for a way to convince her, but she just said a quick and quiet, "Thank you."

Chapter Twelve

Ali trailed Jericho toward the café. He held open the door. After they were seated, she excused herself to the washroom. Grasping the cold sink counter, she searched her reflection. Were her eyes as empty as she felt inside? How terrible was it to mourn a horse more than her own mother? Splashing water didn't improve the puffy redness on her face, nor did it take away the lingering barnyard and manure smells. Yanking paper towels out of the temperamental dispenser, Ali wet them and rubbed the worst of the grime off her forearms.

"This is as good as it gets." She meant to walk out and join Jericho, but her feet didn't move. Why was she here? Alone with *him*. Okay, the café might be pretty full, but it wasn't like Kate or Chance could walk in and interrupt them. She should have stayed at the ranch. There was work to do. Maybe he'd take her back if she asked. Filling up her day with a bunch of tasks would minimize the pain. The hole in her emotions would split open and she would bleed inwardly when she lay in bed tonight, but she'd worry about it then.

As she walked into the eating area, Jericho's blue eyes seemed to drink her in. She tried to remind herself that she didn't like the man with the disarming, crooked grin seated at her table, but that was becoming harder to believe. Honestly, he terrified her—for herself and for what he had the power to do to Chance.

Her trail of thoughts halted when she spied the glass in his hand. An amber liquid with the telltale trace of white froth. Stomach recoiling, she slammed her purse on the table, and he spilled some of the brew on himself. *Serves him right.* She'd been wrong to trust him at all. What was the saying? A leopard always shows his spots. Drunkard. That's all he'd ever be.

Pulling a wad of flimsy napkins from the basket on the table, Jericho dabbed at the wet spot on his shirt. "Got me good." He laughed, and it grated her nerves.

"Hitting the hard stuff a little early, huh?"

"Pardon?"

Giving her best I'm-not-stupid glare, she pointed to his glass.

He stopped dabbing. "You have a problem with that?"

"Yes, actually, I do. *That stuff* ruined our marriage, and you have the audacity to order it and swig it down in front of me like the good old days? Take me home, Jericho." She rose to her feet, but he just leaned back, crossed his arms, and gave her a searching look.

"Taste it."

"What?"

"Taste it."

"You know I don't—"

"Take a drink." He grabbed the glass and thrust it into her hand. She gave a cursory sniff. Well, it didn't smell strong, more sweet, more like… Heat rushed to her face, and Ali set back down the glass as she stumbled into her seat.

Jericho raised a dark eyebrow. "You got something fierce against apple juice? 'Cause if you're gearing up to ask me to sign a petition for some apple cider temperance group, I'm not doing it."

She fanned her face. "You know what I thought."

An emotion filtered across his face, something deep and

sad that made Ali want to take his hand in hers. He straightened back up and rested his arms on the table. "Yes." It came out as a miserable sigh. "I know what you thought. I guess I just wish that wasn't the first thing that came to mind for you."

"I'm sorry." She bowed her head.

"Don't be. In the past, I did nothing but hurt you. You have every right to doubt me. But I promise you, I'm going to do everything in my power to gain back your trust. If it means anything, I haven't touched the stuff in more than five years."

"It's all so weird. You're *supposed* to order a beer. That's the man I remember. But you, like this, I don't know what to do with."

A woman who matched Dolly Parton in voice and hairheight stopped at the table to take their orders. Jericho asked for the chicken club, but Ali declined food.

"Just some iced tea, if you have it."

"Not hungry?" Concern thickened Jericho's voice.

She shook her head.

He cleared his throat. "So you don't know what to do with me, huh?"

"You're so different."

The food arrived, and Jericho bowed his head. Wow, praying in public. That was new, too. When he picked up his silverware and looked at her, an easy peace filled his eyes and made her swallow against her own hollowness.

"Would it be okay? Could I finish what I started telling you at the firework show?"

"That feels like forever ago."

He shook his head. "Just twenty days."

"Come again?"

He gave a little-boy smile, like she'd caught him stealing penny candy. "I've been counting and thanking God for every new day I get with you."

It sounded sincere, sweet even. And that blasted hummingbird came back, banging against her ribs. She narrowed her eyes. "Okay, so talk. I'm listening."

After wiping his mouth with the napkin, he let out a long breath. "It's hard to know where to begin. But I told you about the stuff that happened to me, Yellowstone and the ranches and the army. But I didn't tell you how I changed in here." He touched his chest.

"When that war veteran took me in, he sobered me up. Wouldn't let me leave, and wouldn't let me touch the drink. For a while I was furious. I tried to call the cops on him a couple times, report that he had kidnapped me or something, held me against my will. But then, after the poison got out of my system, it all hit me. I was a coward, and by not facing my troubles, not dealing with the pain in my past, I let it destroy my future, our marriage and I was terrified I'd destroy you."

Ali wanted to say something. Everything in her wanted to ask him why he didn't come home. Why hadn't he been able to work through the issues with her beside him? But she held her tongue.

"Then one day when I mulled it all over, I picked up the guy's Bible and flipped through the worn pages. The first thing I read was this verse telling me that my body is a temple, and I should honor God with it. I made a pact that day that I'd never touch alcohol again, and I haven't."

"Just like that?" Ali snapped her fingers.

"No. It wasn't magical or anything. It was hard work and a lot of almost big-time mess-ups, and yeah, even tears if I'm being honest. But once I got over that, I tried to figure out what to do next. Ali, you've got to understand that at that point I wanted to come home. Badly. I even made all the travel plans, but I couldn't do it."

"Why?" she whispered.

"I wasn't a man worthy of you. In our whole relationship, I only took from you, so I couldn't come home with nothing to offer. I didn't know how to be the husband you needed and deserved. After the stories the vet told me about his time in the army, I decided I'd join and make something of myself, or so the saying goes."

Ali dropped her head into her hands and mumbled, "So like a man."

"Huh?"

"I only ever wanted *you*. I didn't need you to become anything. I just wanted my best friend beside me."

His hand snaked across the table and took hold of hers. With his thumb, he traced circles on her palm while he spoke. "I know. I get that now, but I had this inner drive to prove I was good enough. That, and I didn't think I was ready for the real world. I figured it would be easier to stay sober in the army, but boy was I wrong. It's just like anyplace else. You can find whatever experience you're looking for. It's whatever you want to make of it. So, while the guys went out celebrating, I spent all my time with our chaplain because he was the only person around my age not going out to the bars every free night."

"I'm glad there was someone there for you." The rhythm of his touch to her palm proved too tempting, so she closed her hand around his to make him stop.

"He was. And I told him everything about us and about my life. He didn't do the whole preacher thing on me. He told me that my identity was not the makeup of my past mistakes. He said that I had a clean slate. Man, that changed my world."

"Sounds very convenient though." Ali shrugged away from him. "I mean—what? You're suddenly not accountable for anything in the past? Just—*poof*—pretend it didn't happen?"

"I have to live with a lot of regrets, but I can't let them own the future."

His words reminded Ali of something Kate had told her weeks ago. "You're free."

"I guess I am." The corner of his lip pulled up. "I'm also done with this sandwich. Should we head back?" He looked at his gold watch, once owned by his father. "I think it's been long enough."

As he maneuvered the Jeep out of the parking lot, Ali reviewed their conversation. She tipped her head to watch Jericho out of the corner of her eyes. The man had changed completely; no one could deny that. But then again, he was still her same Jericho. *Her Jericho?* She adjusted her seat belt. Where had that come from? Jericho came back, yes, but not in that way in her life. She had Chance to think about, and Tripp's offer still lingered in her thoughts.

She sighed. Jericho and Tripp. Besides their blue eyes and build, they couldn't be more different. With Jericho, it was like going on the world's biggest, most heart-pounding roller coaster. Tripp? Tripp was the tour bus around the park. But between the two, if an accident occurred, a person was less likely to get hurt on the bus.

It still wasn't okay that Jericho had been gone so long, but she understood his absence a little better now. She couldn't argue the fact that he had become a better man. *Good for him joining the army. Never saw that coming.*

She tensed. As an army man, Jericho was bound to leave her again. Maybe not by choice next time, but did that matter? Even if he wanted to be with her, one day he would leave, and he might never come back. She couldn't—*wouldn't*—open herself or Chance up to that.

"All the streets are blocked off." Jericho rubbed his jaw.

She hadn't been paying attention. But a look down Main Street showed it was empty, and blockades barred the way. Jericho looped the Jeep around in a three-point turn and went down another road.

Ali propped her feet on the dashboard. "Daley Days. With all the commotion, I completely forgot. Looks like they're getting things ready for the street dance this weekend." She loved the celebration that commemorated the town's founder.

"Please tell me they still have the kiss-the-pig contest?" He gave his full-chested laugh as he turned onto the side street that led to her family ranch.

Ali smiled. "Of course! Only the best for our great town."

"Are you taking Chance to all the activities?"

"I really shouldn't. I have a fundraising event for Big Sky Dreams that I need to finish planning, and I'm really not feeling up to it with all that's happened, but I probably will. Chance loves it. What kid wouldn't? We always did."

When he didn't say anything, she looked over and noticed a small, soft smile on his lips. He slung an arm over the steering wheel as they bumped up the gravel driveway.

"What? What are you thinking with that look on your face, Jericho Freed?"

"I like talking to you the way we used to."

When he tossed the Jeep into Park, Kate ran toward them, waving her arms, with Megan and Rider on the front porch. Dread brought a crop of goose bumps to Ali's back. "Oh, no. I think maybe they haven't gotten Denny yet."

Breathless, Kate grabbed Ali's arm the moment she stepped out of the vehicle. "He's gone! We've looked everywhere. We can't find him!" Kate's eyes were wild.

Ali's stomach plummeted.

Jericho rounded the Jeep and laid a hand on Ali's shoulder. "Who's gone, Kate? Spit it out."

"Chance. Chance is missing."

Chapter Thirteen

Jericho's mouth went dry. He worked his jaw back and forth. "What do you mean, *missing?*"

"In all the commotion, he disappeared. One second he was here digging in the mud with Drover, and the next he was gone. We've looked everywhere." Kate wrung her hands. "Megan searched the house. Rider searched the barn, and I looked in the yard."

Ali tore across the driveway toward the house. Screaming her son's name, she burst into her home, running from room to room with Jericho in her wake. Her high-pitched voice echoed up the stairwell. Jericho's heart lurched into his throat. Was Chance prone to wandering off? Ali's terror signaled that it was completely unexpected.

"Chance! C'mon, partner—come out of wherever you're hiding." His loud voice drowned out Ali's.

Her eyes blazed. "Chance Silver! If you are hiding, come out right now. This is not funny." Ali's lip started to tremble, and everything in Jericho wanted to pull her into his arms and make her pain go away. But they needed to find Chance.

He grabbed her and tugged Ali along after him, back toward the yard. Her hand felt cold and clammy, forming a weight in his stomach.

He stopped on the porch and scanned the countryside. "Boys wander. It's just a fact. I used to take off all the time when I was young. I was never in trouble, and I always moseyed back home soon enough."

She worked her bottom lip between her teeth. "Just like you." It was only a whisper, but it made his heart pound harder.

Spinning, he pointed at Kate. "Stay at the house. Check all the rooms again in case he's hiding. Think of places a boy would find neat to explore, like the attic. Megan, stay near the barn and holler if you see him. Rider, take the truck and check out by all the cattle pens. That boy has been more interested in bull riding than I'm comfortable with, and if he decided to try it on his own, you'll find him there. Ali and I will check the rest of the property."

Ali stayed rooted to her spot, her eyes raking over the yard. Jericho placed a hand on the small of her back and propelled her forward. "C'mon, I need action right now, not fear."

She nodded, then started jogging beside him.

Unlatching the corral, he called for Chief. "Is there any other horse here that'll let us ride bareback?"

"Not quickly. The rest are pretty old."

Jericho nodded. Like the old days, he grabbed Chief's mane and hurtled onto the horse. He reached down, grabbed Ali's hand and hoisted her up behind him. When he kicked Chief into motion, she wound her arms around his torso, her cheek pressed against his back. Her tears dampened his shirt.

"Chance!" Making Chief tear across the fields like a young buck, Jericho scanned the horizon. His mind ticked through the options. What on this property would entice a seven-year-old boy? That's where they needed to go.

"I'm so afraid," Ali whispered.

Jericho unwound a hand from Chief's mane and placed it over the one of hers that rested near his heart. "He's just a boy. Don't worry. He's probably off having the time of his life, and we'll laugh about this later."

"But what if someone took him?" Her voice trembled, along with her body.

"Took him? Who would take Chance?"

"Someone is doing bad stuff to the ranch, Jericho. Someone threatened us." Ali wept, her hands fisting the fabric of his shirt. "Chance! Chance, baby, where are you?" Her body shook so much, Jericho worried she'd fall off the horse. Taking Chief hadn't been his best idea, but nothing could get to every nook and cranny of a ranch as quickly as a horse.

"I need you to calm down, Ali."

"Calm down! Didn't you hear me? What if he's been kidnapped? What if... Dear Lord...please don't let anyone hurt him."

A chill ran down Jericho's back. "Think. Where can a kid hide on this property? What place is maybe a bit dangerous? That's where Chance will be."

"The gully."

His stomach dropped. The gully was more than just a bit dangerous. Urging Chief to head west, he took his hand away from Ali and tangled it back into the horse's copper mane. Jericho leaned forward as Chief plunged ahead faster. With each hoof pound bringing the gully closer, Jericho prayed for Chance's safety.

Someone threatened us.

Anger boiled in him. If anyone dared bother Ali, Chance or anyone here, they'd have to answer to him.

Threatened. What on earth could she mean?

Nearing the spot, Jericho slowed the horse's pace. Before he could halt Chief completely, Ali jumped off and raced toward the jagged ravine that split Silver property from Freed property. Jericho leaped down and jogged after her. They yelled the boy's name, scanning the deep niches of the gully. Ali's calls were strangled out between choked sobs, each one wrenching at Jericho's heart. She stumbled on the uneven cliff face, but Jericho caught her around the waist before she fell.

"He's gone," she wailed with her hand cupped over her mouth.

Craning his neck, Jericho hushed her. He thought he heard… *Yep.*

Dropping to his knees, Jericho scooted to the edge of the craggy rocks and looked over. Sure enough. "Right there, Ali. Look, he's down here." He pointed.

Ali lunged forward. Jericho held up his hand to keep her from tumbling off the side.

She swiped the back of her arm over her face. "Where? I don't see him. Chance?"

"Mom!" Chance gulped in air then whined.

"Chance! Chance, baby, come back up here."

"I caaann't." He sniveled.

She squeezed Jericho's arm. "Something's wrong. I think he's hurt."

Reaching out, he cupped the back of Ali's head, making her look him in the eye and hoping she saw something that would make her trust him. "Everything will be okay. I'll go down there and get him. I'll bring him back to you."

Nervous energy prickled his muscles, but he schooled himself not to show it. Jericho licked his lips and dropped his feet over the edge. Growing up at the foot of the Bitterroot Mountains, a man learned to free climb before he could walk. Then again, it had been awhile and he was never all that good at it, but Chance needed him.

He worked the muscles in his jaw. *Find a handhold.* He shifted, fingers shaking as he clung to the cliff face. He wished he'd thought to bring a rope. The rock dug into his skin, but hearing a whimper from where Chance hunched in a crevice pushed Jericho to move faster.

"I'm coming, buddy."

He felt down with his foot, and his toe touched on the small rock shelf beside Chance. Knowing better than to trust the crumble of boulders the boy perched on, Jericho kept a tight hold of the wall as he angled closer. "Hey, bud, you okay?"

Chance shoved out his bottom lip. Red rings circled teary eyes. "My arm hurts. Bad."

"Did you fall in here?"

The boy nodded, and a wash of chills raced down Jericho's spine. He looked up. "Ali. I need you to take Chief and bring back rope."

Her head peeked over the side. "You can't bring Chance up?"

"Not safely. And, Ali, be quick. These rocks are crumbling."

Her head disappeared. Seconds later, Chief's hooves pounded thunder.

Jericho found a small ledge a few feet away and hunkered down. "Your mom'll be back soon. I need you to be very brave, okay?"

Chance peeked at him. "But my arm."

"Why were you down here, anyway?"

"Megan said there were kittens crying by the gully. I heard her tell Aunt Kate."

Jericho dragged in a long breath. "And you didn't like to think of them stuck in here, did you?"

"No. What if they couldn't find their mom?"

Jericho craned his neck, but didn't hear any mews.

A truck roared across the field. Rider's head appeared over the gully wall. "Mr. Freed?"

"Rider. We need help."

"Me and Miss Ali brought some rope. I'm going to tie it to one of these trees and toss it down."

A cable snaked over the edge of the cliff face, and Ali dropped another bunch of rope down the ledge. Jericho caught it and gingerly worked his way over to where Chance stooped.

He constructed a makeshift climber's harness around

I accept your offer!

Please send me two free Love Inspired® novels and two mystery gifts (gifts worth about $10). I understand that these books are completely free— even the shipping and handling will be paid—and I am under no obligation to purchase anything, ever, as explained on the back of this card.

❏ I prefer the regular-print edition
105/305 IDL FVZH

❏ I prefer the larger-print edition
122/322 IDL FVZH

Please Print

FIRST NAME

LAST NAME

ADDRESS

APT.#   CITY

STATE/PROV.   ZIP/POSTAL CODE

Visit us online at
www.ReaderService.com

Offer limited to one per household and not applicable to series that subscriber is currently receiving.

Your Privacy—The Harlequin® Reader Service is committed to protecting your privacy. Our Privacy Policy is available online at www.ReaderService.com or upon request from the Harlequin Reader Service. We make a portion of our mailing list available to reputable third parties that offer products we believe may interest you. If you prefer that we not exchange your name with third parties, or if you wish to clarify or modify your communication preferences, please visit us at www.ReaderService.com/consumerchoice or write to us at Harlequin Reader Service Preference Service, P.O. Box 9062, Buffalo, NY 14269. Include your complete name and address.

LI-GF-13   ◄ Detach card and mail today. No stamp needed ►   ◄ © 2012 HARLEQUIN ENTERPRISES LIMITED. ® and ™ are trademarks owned and/or used by the trademark owner and/or its licensee. Printed in the U.S.A.

Chance then, binding it with more knots than necessary, he attached it to the dangling rope. "I know your arm hurts, but I need you to be really strong, okay? I need you to hold on tight, even if it hurts and you want to let go." He tugged the rope, certain it would hold. "Rider, go on and hoist him up."

He patted Chance's head. "You're secure, but I still want you to hang on to this rope like it's that bull you always wanted to ride."

Chance bit his lip and nodded.

Jericho smiled and lifted his chin. "Win the buckle, kid."

Swirling her cup of lukewarm coffee, Ali leaned back against the cool hospital wall.

Jericho layed down the magazine he'd been reading. "What's the verdict?"

She sighed. It had been a long day. First with Denny, then an emotional conversation with Jericho, then Chance—her heart seized. She should have been there. "He broke his wrist. They're casting it right now. He picked the camo plaster because he wanted to match you, Mr. Army."

"Thank God that's all it was."

Sliding into the waiting room chair, she set down her coffee. "Do you need a doctor, Jericho? Were you injured climbing? I saw you limping afterward."

"I'm fine. I'm more worried about you."

She sipped her coffee. "Me? I'm not the one who free-climbed into the gully."

"What did you mean earlier, when you said someone's threatening you?"

"I don't really want to talk about it."

"Ali." He grabbed her hand. "Remember, I promised to protect you. If someone has done something that makes you think Chance could have been in danger of being kidnapped, then I need to know."

How much to tell him? *The truth.* She swallowed hard.

"Things have been happening around the ranch lately that make me think someone is trying to harm me."

His eyebrows knit together. "What sort of things?"

"Money is missing from the Big Sky Dreams account, and someone has been tampering with our fences and letting out the cattle. We lost three heifers in the ravine so far. You knew that someone slashed my tires. The horses were set loose twice now. And I found a note."

"A note?"

"Yeah, someone left a creepy note tacked to my door saying that if I valued what was important to me, I'd stay away from you." She twisted the lid on the coffee cup.

"From me? It named me specifically?"

She nodded. "It said something about seeing us together at the Independence Day Picnic. That I'd been warned."

He rubbed his thumb over the top of her clenched knuckles. "Why didn't you tell me sooner?"

"Because it's not your problem." Ali jerked her hand from his and crossed her arms.

"If I'm named as the reason these things are happening to you, then I'm already involved."

"If I had told you, would you have stayed away?"

"Absolutely not. I'd have been around more, like I'll be now. We'll get to the bottom of it. I'll figure out who's behind it and—"

"Hey, Mom. Hey, Jericho." Chance crossed the room with a nurse at his side. "Look how cool this is. I could hide in the woods, and no one would see me. Will you both sign my arm?"

Jericho's laugh failed to calm Ali. The tight lines around his eyes were still present, and she knew they meant trouble for her. He wasn't about to drop their conversation about the note. If she heard him right, he was about to say he'd take care of whoever wanted to cause them harm. But that didn't sit well with her, because she didn't want Jericho in danger either.

* * *

How the fool man convinced her to come out to the street dance, Ali had no idea. She shook her head as she walked beside Jericho. The rowdy twang of country music filled the air. Laughter and the clips of boots against Main Street bounced off the buildings lining downtown.

Chance cupped his cast and looked at Jericho with round eyes. "Can I ride on your back?"

"Sure thing, partner." He bent down so her son could scramble up. He grunted. "Watch the kidneys, kid."

Chance scooped off Jericho's hat, giving it a new home swimming over his small head. She smiled at the way Jericho's hair stuck up in all directions, but the rough-and-tumble look only increased his appeal. The man looked too tempting for his own good—clean-shaven, in his pressed denim shirt and muscle-hugging jeans.

The sun would dip behind the Bitterroot Mountains in the next hour, but warmth remained for the black tank top and gauzy skirt she'd donned. Ali always liked the way boots looked with a knee-length skirt, especially while twirling during a country dance.

As if reading her mind, Jericho glanced over. "I'm glad they've kept this a family thing. Real friendly, with all the old-timers and kids involved."

She smoothed down her hair and moved toward the sidewalk, away from the crowd already line dancing. "They've stayed pretty true to the innocent olden days."

"Hey, look." Jericho jutted out his chin. "There are Kate and Rider dancing together. When he's not working, that guy sure follows her around like a homeless hound dog. Is something going on between them?"

"I sure hope not." Making sure Chance wasn't paying attention, Ali leaned close and whispered, "We think Rider might be our saboteur."

Jericho laughed. "Rider Longley? Absolutely not. He loves your family."

"I've heard differently."

He shot her a look that said they'd talk about it later.

Up front near where the deejay and square-dance callers stood, children of all ages moved to the beat. While most knew the steps, one freckle-faced boy spun in helter-skelter circles, ricocheting off other dancers.

Chance tapped Jericho on the head. "Will you take me up there?"

"Sure thing, pal."

"Will you stay and dance with me?"

Jericho yanked on his collar and widened his eyes at Ali. He mouthed, *Save me.*

She laughed. The cowboy had never been much for dancing, but he could use a little torture all the same. "I think that's a great idea, Chance. You and Jericho go on up there, and I'm going to find me some huckleberry lemonade."

"You owe me!" Jericho called over his shoulder with a full-chested laugh.

She liked that about him—when he laughed, he did it completely, none of that chuckling stuff. Pulling out of the crowd, she took in the sight of all her friends and neighbors enjoying the evening. A teen with long black hair slow-danced with arms fully extended, swaying side to side. A father with dimples danced with his daughter perched on his toes.

Ali's eyes lingered on an elderly couple, gnarled hands entwined over their hearts as they barely shuffled to the music together. At the song's crescendo, the elderly man leaned forward and kissed his little white-puff-haired wife right on her firecracker-red lips.

Ali's eyes welled up at the sight. A lump the size of Montana formed in her throat, as if all her bitterness and regrets had risen and now she wanted them gone. She wanted freedom from the weeds growing like manacles, restraining her heart from hope and forgiveness. She wanted love like *that*.

Sliding her gaze, she bit down a laugh. Good to his word, Jericho stood up front surrounded by a crowd of kids, attempting to dance and making a complete and adorable fool of himself. As if embarrassed, Chance kept stopping him, and then he'd demonstrate a move and make a hand motion inviting Jericho to try. Jericho looked more like he was trying to shake a prairie dog off his back than any dancing Ali had ever seen.

"Care to dance?" Tripp touched the small of her back.

"Tripp. You startled me." She spilled a bit of her lemonade onto the straw bales lining the street. She surveyed the tanned lawyer. "I didn't know you owned boots."

He shrugged. "The event seemed to call for them. Got your attention turned elsewhere, I see." He jutted his chin in Jericho's direction.

"Yeah, Chance broke his arm a couple days ago so I want to keep a close eye on him."

"Are you okay? I heard about Denny."

Tears stung Ali's eyes. She shook her head.

"I understand if you don't want to talk, but I want you to know I'm here if you need anything. I'll do anything for you, Alison. You know that, right?" He flashed a made-for-Hollywood smile.

"You've been such a good friend to me these last few years. I don't know what I would have done without you."

"I haven't seen you out there yet." He took the cup from her hand and set it down on the steps leading to the bakery door. "Mind if I'm the first tonight?" He offered his hand.

Ali shrugged. "I guess that would be fine." With the rest of her family occupied, a dance with a friend sounded harmless. Although, Tripp didn't just want to be her friend, did he? Ali swallowed hard, regretting accepting his hand already.

* * *

Jericho froze and watched that man pull *his wife* out onto the street. Tripp put one of his hands on Ali's slender waist. Then he entwined his fingers with hers. Tripp looked up, meeting Jericho's stare. He gave Jericho a crooked smile, then turned his face into Ali's hair.

"Jericho." Chance tapped his arm. "I think you're too old for this because your face is all red, and the vein on your neck looks like it's going to pop out. You should sit."

Scooping his hat off the kid's head, Jericho took a few deep breaths to calm himself enough for rational thought. "You're right, Chance. I need to slow down a bit, but I'm not sitting this one out. Not on my life." He stalked through the crowd, bumping into a couple and making them miss their dance steps. "Sorry," he muttered. Nothing would deter his course. Not when it concerned Ali. He'd fight for her until she told him flat-out to stop.

Zeroing in on the pair, he tapped her on the shoulder. "Mind if I cut in?"

Tripp scoffed. "Actually, we do."

"I asked the lady."

Both men looked at Ali. She bit her lip. "It's okay, Tripp. Thanks for the dance."

Jericho puffed out his chest, heart swelling. He took Ali's hands and pulled her against him.

The corners of her mouth twitched as if she fought a smile. "You shouldn't have done that. An angry Tripp isn't worth one dance."

"Don't like seeing another man with his mugs on my wife." Holding her this close, he whispered against her ear. The silky strands of her hair tickled his mouth. He shut his eyes.

She trembled against him.

He pressed her closer. "Shhh. It's okay, Ali. Please be with me like this."

"Jericho...I'm not... You can't..."

The pain in his knee made their dance more like a shuffle-stop-walk, but he didn't care. "I want it to be just you and me, Ali. I've always wanted that."

She pushed back a little, but still in his arms. "It's not just me anymore. I have Chance. We're a package deal."

He stopped dancing and tipped her chin to hold her gaze as he spoke. "I want you both."

"But what if—"

He put a hand on either side of her neck, cradling the back of her head with his fingers. "I don't care who his father is, Ali. He's your son. But if you let me, I'd love him like he was mine."

"Even if…?"

"In fact, I might already."

Her eyes searched his. "You do?"

"Of course I do." He smiled, waiting for her to open up and confirm that Chance was his son. Instead, she nodded once and laid her head back on his shoulder.

Jericho sighed. Maybe in time she'd trust him enough to tell him the truth.

Chapter Fourteen

"I hardly think it's necessary for you to stay here." Ali jammed her hands to her hips and tapped her foot against the floor.

Kate wrinkled her brow. "I don't know, Al. I think it's wise to have a man here until stuff blows over."

Ali shot her sister a glare. *Traitor.*

"It won't work. We don't have any extra beds so—"

Jericho shook his head. "While in the army, I learned to sleep anywhere. I slept leaning against a tank wheel in the middle of mortar fire once. I could curl up on the kitchen tile in there and be just fine."

Chance slurped on the last of his firecracker Popsicle. Blue and red colors painted his face. "That's gross. You could sleep in my room, but my bed is small. Mom said I'll get a bigger one soon, though." He looked up at Ali with hopeful eyes, as if she'd spring for a new bed after his benevolent offer to Jericho.

"Appreciate that, but this couch in here will work just fine."

"Yeah, I don't need you in my room 'cause I'm strong. I'm a guy." Chance chewed on the Popsicle stick, thinking hard. "You should sleep in Mom's room with her. She's got a big bed."

Kate ducked, hiding a chuckle behind her hand.

Heat crept up Ali's neck, but seeing the full-out fire on Jericho's cheeks made her feel better. "Enough, Chance. Get upstairs, wash your face and throw on your jammies." She pointed toward the stairs.

The boy set down the stick on the coffee table. When he faced Jericho, he shrugged. "I'm just saying. I'm brave, but she's a girl, and girls get scared easy. And she has the biggest bed. It makes sense."

"Put it like that, and it sure does make sense. But between you and me, I think it's safer for everyone if I'm down here on the couch." He shot Ali a look.

"To bed, Chance."

He harrumphed but obeyed, albeit with loud, drawn-out steps on the stairs.

Ali chuckled. "I'll be up in ten minutes to read the first chapter of that book with you. Be ready when I come."

Jericho set down his cup of milk and stretched. "You know what? I'm going to go up there and search all the rooms."

"You can't be serious." Ali inched toward the stairs to block his progress.

He took her shoulders and gently moved her aside. "Listen. When we were looking for Chance, you really believed that someone might have taken him. If you're that afraid of whatever is going on, then yes, I'm going to take it seriously. And I'm going to go up and check all the rooms so I know for sure that nothing's lurking that shouldn't be."

Lurking? She hadn't thought of that. Now she wouldn't get a wink of sleep. She stepped back. "When you put it like that…"

He disappeared up the stairs.

"You okay with all this?" Kate dropped down on the couch, sprawling her feet on the coffee table.

Ali sunk into the side chair. "Not like you offered much help."

"Oh, c'mon. You know that having him here is probably the best thing right now. Who's going to try to mess with the ranch when they find out he's standing guard?"

"I just... It's not proper."

"Proper? He's your husband. What could be more proper?"

Ali leaned her head on the overstuffed armrest. "I haven't slept under the same roof with that man in more than eight years. It's unnerving. I was just getting used to him being back in my life. But not like this, not all the time and not in our house."

A devilish smile pulled at Kate's lips as a mocking gleam lit her eyes. "Well, if Chance had his way, your husband would be...*in your bed.*"

Ali burst out laughing. "What am I going to do with that child? He's set on pairing us up. I was mortified."

Kate crossed her arms over her stomach and closed her eyes. "You sure you're okay?"

"Besides this stuff, I'm pretty stressed out for the 'Dream A Little Dream' event I have for Big Sky Dreams. I mean, if we don't get the money, I don't know what we're going to do. And this is the first event we're having here on our property." Her sister nodded off, so Ali stopped talking.

Finishing the last of her water, Ali looked up at the ceiling, listening for footsteps. Silence. Ali crossed her legs, jiggling her foot. How long did it take to peek into a couple of rooms? Losing the battle with her curiosity, she tiptoed past Kate and crept upstairs. A small sliver of light trickled from under Chance's bedroom door, but not enough to illuminate the hallway. Shadows painted the second floor. Ali peered into her bedroom. Negative. Then she turned the corner at the end of the hall and gasped.

Oh no! Jericho Freed stood in *that* room. An unwritten rule in the house was that the door to that room, the small room at the back of the house, stayed shut at all times. Her heart pounded so loud, it reverberated in her ears. He shouldn't be in there.

She stayed in the hall, grabbing the cool door handle for support. She was thankful, at least, that Jericho's back was to her. Ali cleared her throat, nice and loud. "Are you done checking the rooms?"

When he whirled around, Ali noticed that it looked like he was trying very hard to keep his composure. "All my stuff. You kept everything," he whispered.

She gave what she hoped came off as an indifferent shrug. "It was that or toss the junk."

Jericho rubbed his jaw, then reached out and trailed his fingers over a box full of his old paperback Westerns. "But you kept it. For eight years. Why?"

Giving a little growl, Ali stalked to the stairs. "I don't know, Jericho. Just leave me be about it. And get out. That door is supposed to stay closed."

He brushed past her, his voice husky. "But it's open now."

Crunch.

Okay. The first sound could have been his imagination, but that one? No, that was real. Stealing across the grass, it whooshed a bit in the still night as Jericho investigated the source of the noise. With deliberate steps, he came to the front of the barn and craned his neck to listen.

The sound—a horse, maybe? Blame it on a year experiencing the harsh realities of war, but Jericho Freed didn't like to leave a strange noise unexplored. Sure, that same fact cost him his army career, but this was Ali's safety. He wasn't about to take any chances.

His fingers grazed the barn door. Just as he feared. *Unlatched.* With it hanging open, he squeezed his body through then faded into the shadowed area near the stall doors.

He squinted into the darkness. A person in dark clothes hunched over something in the stall used for storing hay. A chill washed over him. Ali was right. No other explanation existed for someone being in the barn at this time of night. Despite the slicing pain in his knee, Jericho pressed against the wall and slunk toward the wrongdoer. His footfalls undetected, he grabbed the dark figure by the arm and flung the intruder around to face him, pressing them hard against the wall.

Jericho clamped his hand over the perpetrator's mouth. "I'm gonna lift my hand in a minute, and you're going to tell me two things. Why are you here? And why are you hassling Ali?" As he spoke, his eyes adjusted to the darkness, and recognition poured through him. He took the slender but firm arm in his hand, the petite frame and long, dark hair. "Megan?"

She shoved away his hand from her face and wiped her mouth with her sleeve. "Of course. What are you doing here?"

Peering around her into the stall, Jericho saw three gas cans, an ax and some rope. He narrowed his eyes at her. "What are *you* doing?"

She ran a hand over her hair. "Didn't Ali tell you?"

"Tell me what?"

"Huh. Guess she doesn't trust you."

"I'm calling the cops."

"Easy there, Trigger. I'm doing a stakeout. Helping Ali catch the person who's been doing stuff."

He raised his eyebrows. "Which is why you're putting gas in a highly flammable room? Are you crazy? There's hay dust everywhere. This place is one step from an inferno."

"I will have you know—" she crossed her arms and stepped away from him "—that Rider Longley left these next to the house. Pretty suspicious, if you ask me. I was moving them, and I didn't think it was dangerous in here. It's just hay dust." She shrugged.

Jericho grabbed her biceps in one hand, and the can of

gasoline in the other. "I don't buy a word of this. Let's go see if Ali gives the same story."

He dragged her with more force than necessary across the yard and up the front steps. A wild, howling fear bit at his ankles the entire walk to the house. Rope? Gasoline? An ax? At least now the gas can was clear of the hay dust.

"How do you know Rider left that stuff near the house?"

"Who else? He's the one with a vendetta against this family. Will you *let me go?*" She shoved at his hand as they tripped up the porch steps.

Jericho thought about the implications of the items Megan found. Who made a big to-do about always carrying matches? *Tripp.* It all made sense. The letter—he was at the Independence Day picnic. He didn't want Ali near Jericho. He probably banked on the fact that Ali would run into his arms for protection. *Think again, Tripp Phillips.* Jericho wasn't about to let that happen.

He released Megan, and they entered the house.

Ali bolted from her chair. The book she'd been reading tumbled to the ground. "Megan? Is something wrong? What are you doing here?"

He spoke before Megan could. "Is Megan supposedly trying to help you stake out the place?"

Ali looked slowly from him to Megan and then back to him. "We had talked about it. Yes. Trying to catch Rider."

"That's all I need to know." He turned to Megan. "Sorry if I scared you, but I had to be sure."

"Whatever. I'll see you both tomorrow. Sorry for trying to help." Megan elbowed past him, her voice dripping sarcasm.

Ali trailed Megan out to the porch. "Hey, wait up."

Her friend turned, palming at her cheeks.

"What just happened?"

"Are you going to marry Tripp? I heard, that night when he asked you in the kitchen."

Megan's question jarred Ali like a bear trap crushing her leg. Marry Tripp? She didn't want to think about that right now.

She sighed. "I don't know."

"Why not? I mean, Tripp's a good guy."

"You're right, Tripp's an amazing guy. He's been there for me when I had no one. He's been my closest friend the past couple years."

"But you're already married."

Ali's shoulders slumped, and she looked out at the mountains. Married? Okay, but only in the legal sense, really. "You're technically right."

"I think you should stay with your husband." Megan rubbed her hands up and down her arms. The evening carried a distinct chill, despite how hot the day had been.

Ali swallowed hard. "You do?"

"He's a nice guy. I don't know what happened between you two in the past, but he cares about you, Ali. You should have seen the way he rounded on me in that barn when he thought I was there to do something nefarious. He loves you."

Later, with those words etched in her mind, Ali stared up at the ceiling of her bedroom, unable to sleep. Drover gave a giant puppy yawn and eased tighter against her in the bed. She turned and splayed her hands into the dog's silken fur, running his floppy ears through her fingers as he gave a little harrumph and closed his eyes.

"I don't know if I can handle it all. Do You hear me, God? It's too much," she whispered. But it didn't feel like the prayer penetrated the walls, let alone made it all the way to heaven.

The ache in her heart had begun as a throb the moment she was alone. Now, hours later, it felt like open heart surgery without anesthesia. Denny was gone. *Dead. Forever.* Someone was after her. Jericho was here. Ali squeezed her eyes shut.

She felt like a pocket turned inside out with nothing left to give. Using the edge of her blanket, she dabbed at the tears sliding down her cheek, hoping the sniffling wasn't as loud as it felt. Ali turned into Drover, using his back to muffle the sobs that threatened to rake through her body at any moment.

Bolting up, Jericho's gaze scanned the room. The bags of frozen veggies he'd put on his knees slid to the floor with a plop. With the steps of a practiced hunter, he stole to the stairs and heard a sound that made the hairs on the back of his neck prickle. The subdued moan came from upstairs. *If anyone hurt Ali, or Chance, or Kate...*

He took the stairs two at a time. Bending an ear near each door, he listened for the haunting sound again. All he heard were soft snores from Kate's room. Nothing by Chance's, so he pushed open the door. The child lay sprawled on his bed, his chest rising and falling with deep sleep. Jericho backed out of the room. Finding Ali's ajar, he peeked in, and his heart constricted. No evil Tripp stood over the bed with an ax, but the sight of Ali crying sickened him all the same.

Leaning against the wall in the hallway, he prayed for guidance and for Ali's peace. She sniffled, and his gut told him to do something to help her. Without thinking, he went back downstairs and put on the cast iron kettle. As the water warmed, he fumbled through the drawers and the pantry looking for mint tea. While they were married, Ali had experienced trouble sleeping. The only remedy had been mint tea—and him rubbing circles on her back until she drifted off.

Regret formed a lump in his throat. How had she fallen to sleep after he left? Lost in the alcohol, he'd never thought about it before, and the totality of what his leaving had done to her rocked through him.

Hands shaking, he poured a cup and let it steep.

The floorboard creaked behind him. Dressed in oversized sweats, Ali blinked. "What are you doing?"

Jericho crossed the room and held out the cup to her. "It's mint. I heard you crying."

She bowed her head and took the cup, blowing on the warm liquid before sipping. "You remembered."

"'Course I did. I haven't forgotten anything about you." He motioned for her to join him at the table. "Do you need anything else?"

"No." She straightened. "I should go back to sleep."

He sighed. "I'm here…whenever you need me."

Ali surveyed him through the rising steam. Her eyes searched him, almost caressing his face. Cautiously, Jericho took a step forward and pressed a kiss to her forehead. "Sleep well."

As she left the room, he heard a very quiet "Thank you."

Chapter Fifteen

"Please, Mom, please." Chance's dress shoes left skid marks on the clean kitchen floor as he hopped up and down.

Ali scrubbed the same serving platter with a Brillo pad for the third time. "Oh, I don't know. There's so much to get done around here, and if you all are leaving, I'll need to do double time."

Kate captured the plate and yanked it away, rescuing it from another round of scouring. "If you don't want to come to church with us, it's okay, Al. Just say so, and everyone will leave you alone."

The scrape of Jericho's chair as he pushed back from the table drew everyone's attention. He nodded his head once, real slow. It seemed to be some sort of secret signal because Kate grabbed Chance's hand and headed out the back door.

Ali wrung her hands, puckered from dishwater.

Jericho rose and clomped toward her. All dressed up in a tucked-in button-down, a tie and suit coat—but the jeans and boots still screamed cowboy. "No one's interested in forcing you to do anything you don't want to. You know that, right?"

She bobbed her head.

He came closer. The spicy, woodsy trace of his cologne drifted over her, and she fought the urge to close her eyes and breathe deeply—that, or bury her nose against that place on his neck where she knew he sprayed the enticing nectar.

She swung toward the oven and snatched the dirty skillet.

He followed her. "I wanted to thank you for letting me bring Chance with me today. Thank you for trusting me with him."

She batted hair from her eyes. "He's thrilled to go."

He eased the skillet out of her hand and dropped it into the sink. A little water sloshed onto the counter. When he reached for the dishcloth, she leaned out of his way. He mopped up the spill on the counter, then dropped the cloth into the dirty dishwater.

She looked down, straightening the rug with her foot. "I want to go, too." She met his eyes—his soft, pleading eyes. "I know it's stupid, but I feel like God will shoot lightning bolts at the church or something if I dare to darken the doors."

His lips creased into an easy smile. "It'd be more like fireworks celebrating a daughter's homecoming. But I understand. I've felt that way before."

With a sigh, she rubbed her elbow. "It would just feel strange walking in there, after all this time."

"They're holding the worship service in the park today in lieu of a church gathering. And so far, it looks like God hasn't tampered with you whenever you're outside, so I think you'll be in the clear today." Jericho winked.

"It's out in the park?"

"You can get up and walk away if you feel uncomfortable."

"I think I'll come, then. Shouldn't you guys have left already?"

"If Kate's hot to trot she can leave, but I'll wait. I'll always wait for you."

Her eyes locked with Jericho's. He thought she was worth waiting for. Warmth flooded through her, and suddenly she couldn't think of another reason in the world to stay away from him.

* * *

On the drive over, Jericho eased her discomfort. He promised the service would be casual, and he complimented her outfit twice. When the Jeep halted in the parking spot, she looked down at her white capris, strappy sandals and sapphire V-neck crew. A necklace or some sort of embellishment would have been nice, but it had been the best she could scrounge up in seven minutes.

Jericho rounded the car and opened the door for her, offering his hand to assist her down. "Don't want you twisting an ankle in your fancy shoes."

"They don't even have heels." She took his hand all the same.

Chance bounded over from the truck Kate drove. His tie was already missing, and his sleeves were rolled to his elbows. "Mom, Aunt Kate says we get to sit on the ground and that there will be cake and juice afterward." He caught her hand and swung it as they picked their way through the crowd together.

Jericho's laugh washed over them. "Church isn't outside all the time, bud, but they do usually have treats after service."

The group located an open spot on the side of the gathering. Before they sat down, Jericho shrugged out of his suit coat and laid it on the ground, motioning for Ali to sit on it while the band on the platform started singing.

Her eyes widened. "I don't want to get your coat dirty."

One side of his lips lifted, and something twinkled in his eyes. "I don't want your white pants getting ruined."

"Good point." She lowered herself onto his coat. He did the same and edged closer. Chance plopped down on her other side, and Kate sat on some grass at the end of the line.

When the service ended, Ali rose and gathered Jericho's coat in her arms. Before she could bolt to the Jeep, neighbors swarmed her with hugs.

Mrs. Casey, one of Ali's high school teachers, squeezed

tight. "You dear thing. Why, I'm so pleased to see you out today. Does a heart good to see my old students. And who might this strapping young man be?" She peered at Chance over her glasses. Ali introduced them.

"Is that Alison Silver?" Linda Smeer, a sleepover sister from days gone by, shook Ali by her shoulders. "I can't believe it. I'm so excited to see you. I think about stopping by your ranch all the time, but I know you're so busy. Let's plan a time to catch up."

"I'd love that." Ali smiled at her, and they exchanged cell phone numbers.

Two families with students in her program stepped forward and greeted her. Ali swapped a high five with Ned. He'd come a long way since joining the Big Sky Dreams program. Seeing him so comfortable around the large crowd, and able to handle contact, made moisture gather in her eyes.

Jericho poked her in the side, his eyebrows raised. He offered her a red velvet cupcake from the dessert table. "Looks like you've got a lot of friends here."

She plucked at the wrapper. "More than I realized. I think next week I'll come to church with you guys again, even if it's inside the building. I've missed this."

"No lightning?"

"Not yet." She couldn't help the smile that bloomed on her face. Nor the sigh that escaped after she bit into the delicious treat.

Jericho patted Salsa's neck and checked the horse's water. Full. Good. A barn cat slunk into the stable. He scooped up the furry intruder, then latched the door shut.

"Don't let Drover see that you found the cat," Ali called from down the line. He watched her. She stopped near the empty fifth stall and trailed her fingers over the door. Denny's stall. Ali wrapped her arms around her middle and turned away.

Jericho picked up his speed. "Anything else need doing?"

She pressed her lips together. "No. All the horses are in and fed. We just lock up the barn, then I spend some time with Chance before bed."

"He challenged me to a game of Battleship." He set the cat near the tower of hay bales.

They walked together out of the barn, and Ali stopped to turn the lock. She checked twice to make certain the door was secure. "Are you prepared to be sunk? He's insanely good at it."

He caught her gaze and held tight. The gold flecks in the hazel pools shimmered. *Sunk? More like hook, line and sinker. What are you doing to me, Ali?* He cleared his throat. "So what's on the menu for dessert tonight?"

"I made cookies-and-cream cupcakes earlier. They should be cool now, so they only need frosting. They'll be ready by the time your ships are destroyed."

"Such a vote of confidence."

"Oh, you don't know how Chance gets when he's playing board games."

He rubbed the stubble on his chin and laughed. "You forget. I've lost to him in Clue twice now."

Looking out across the corral, Ali crossed her arms and sighed.

He touched her hand. "What's on your mind?"

"Sometimes I wonder if starting Big Sky Dreams was one enormous mistake. I mean, it takes so much of my time away from Chance. Not just the lessons, but I spend so much time looking for donations and planning fundraisers, too. I wonder sometimes if it's all worth it."

"You take good care of Chance. Don't doubt that."

She started walking toward the house again, and he fell into step with her.

Ali gave a quick nod. "You know you don't have to keep staying here. I'm sure you're needed at your dad's place."

"I'm not. His staff took care of the place before I came home, and they can take care of it just fine without me." Jericho grabbed the front door, holding it open for her. She smiled at him, and his heart hammered against his rib cage. The past week spent around her only strengthened his determination to win back his wife. "Believe me, I'm right where I'm supposed to be."

Chapter Sixteen

Ali waved as her last student left, then wiped her hands on her jeans. With the "Dream A Little Dream" fundraising event tomorrow, she needed to finish polishing all the tack, make the barn shine and hose down a couple of the dustier horses. Beyond that, calling vendors for confirmation and checking to make certain the attractions she planned to offer to donors were set ranked top on her list for today.

Chance popped up beside her elbow. "Know what, Mom?"

She smiled. In his scuffed black boots, jeans and T-shirt, the bandanna tied around his neck *like Jericho's* made him look like a cowboy-in-training. "What, Mr. Chance?"

"I reminded Jericho about camping, and he said we can go this weekend, as long as you say it's okay." He jumped beside her as he talked.

"Did he, now?" Ali rolled the ends of a set of reins in her left hand. "How much work have you accomplished today?"

"We did everything you asked. Cleared all the weeds, and Jericho mowed the yard. I swept the porch, and I even helped Megan rake the corral. It is *so* clean, Mom."

She layed down the tack and walked to the barn entrance, pretending to scrutinize her crew's work. To be honest, the property hadn't looked better since before Dad died. The guests for tomorrow's event would find Big Sky Dreams shining with a professional polish.

She turned back to her son. "Everything looks amazing. So you win. It's okay with me if you go camping with Jericho this weekend."

"Aren't you coming?"

"Oh, honey, I think it'll be better if just you two boys go." Jericho proved capable enough and trustworthy. She could relax with Chance under his care for one night. And besides, it would give her some time away from the man's intoxicating presence that threatened to throw her well-planned life off-course.

Yes. She welcomed any excuse to get him away for a while, even if that included time alone with her son. Which frightened her too, but somehow she trusted Jericho not to tell Chance about their marriage now—even more than she trusted herself around him.

"You hafta come. It won't be fun without you." He grabbed her hand and tugged a little, yanking her toward the corral. Jericho crouched nearby, giving the fence a new coat of white paint. "Jericho!" Chance bounced on the balls of his feet. "She said we can go camping. But she said she won't come with us."

He took off his hat and scratched his head. "Not coming?"

"I thought it would be good if you guys went alone, made it just a boys' thing."

"You have to talk her into going. I'd even help with the fence. See, Mom." Chance grabbed Jericho's abandoned brush and smeared the next post so the paint ran down in goopy globs.

"Aw. Come with us. We want you there." Jericho cocked an arm on the rail, tilting his head to her with a half smile. "I think it'd be good, the three of us together."

"I just think it's better—"

Chance jumped back to his feet, flinging a long stream

of paint across the lawn. "Who will tuck me in if you're not there?"

"Well, Jericho, I guess."

"He can't. Only a mom can do it. That's the rules. You have to come."

"Hey, Al? I need you over here," Kate called from the maintenance barn.

Ali cupped her hands around her mouth. "One second, Kate!" She turned back to Chance and plucked the dripping brush from his hand. "You are so helpful, sweetheart. Could you maybe use just a little less paint?"

Jericho appropriated the tool and winked at her. "I'll show him how to do it. This'll be the best fence from here to Canada. What do you say, Chance?"

Her son scratched his chin. "Probably."

Shaking her head, Ali bit back a chuckle. She started to walk away, but a cold damp tickle went up her arm. She looked down at the white stripe. "Aw. Sick, Jericho." She swatted at him. His eyes gleamed with mischief. "This is outdoor paint. It'll take forever to wash off."

"I know." He bit back a laugh.

Ali scooped at the dollop running down her arm and raised an eyebrow at him. He backed up, bumping into the wet fence. When he craned to look at the damage to the back of his shirt, Ali smeared her handful across his jaw and neck.

He pounced, missing her. She squealed and took off running. His full-chested laugh echoed after her. She glanced over her shoulder and smirked. Jericho turned his attention back to Chance, smearing two streaks like war paint onto her son's cheeks.

She reached the run-down green barn panting. It housed broken equipment and old, busted tack. Rustic to the core, no modern conveniences graced the old building. The only light trickling in came from cracks in the side walls and holes in the roof. Birds roosted on the rafters. Ali hated the maintenance barn and avoided going inside it. But it also housed the large wagon occasionally used to give hay rides to the Big Sky Dreams students. She planned to offer rides to donors tomorrow, so she plunged into the musty building.

Squinting to locate Kate among the piles of unwanted items, Ali found her sister on her hands and knees next to the wagon.

"Need something?"

From her prone position, Kate huffed, then sat back on the heels of her feet. "What were you talking about with Chance and Jericho?"

"I said they could go camping this weekend, and they were trying to convince me to go along. I don't think it's a good idea." She rubbed at the smear on her elbow.

"Al, your family wants you. Why would you say no to that?"

"My *family?*"

"Your husband and son. What else would you call that?"

Tracing her fingertips along the grooved wood on the side of the wagon, Ali shrugged. "Just sounds weird." She straightened. "You didn't call me over to ask me that, did you?"

Kate paused. "No. When was the last time you looked at this thing?"

Ali worked her bottom lip between her teeth. "Yesterday morning. Why?"

"'Cause you can't use it. The axle's busted."

Dropping down beside her sister, Ali craned her neck to look under the wagon. Sure enough, the back axle hung in two splinted pieces. "But I checked every inch of this thing yesterday. It wasn't like that. Kate, it looks like…like someone *sawed* through the axle."

"That's what I thought, too."

Fear, now a gnawing companion, ignited Ali's nerves. "Who would do such a thing?"

"Besides us, who has keys to the barn?"

"Only..."

"Rider." They spoke the name in unison.

Charging from the barn, Ali spotted Tripp Phillips climbing out of his Subaru. She called to him. A lawyer was exactly what she needed. With quick, long strides, they met each other midway in the yard. From the corner of her eye, she saw Jericho stop talking to Chance and stand, watching her. At least he remained out of earshot. He'd flip if he knew about the wagon.

Tripp placed his hands on her shoulders and squeezed. "What's wrong, Alison? You look like you've seen a ghost."

"I might as well have. Someone's been doing stuff, really bad stuff, to the ranch and—"

"Doing stuff to the ranch? Why didn't I know about this?" His grip tightened. "Are you okay? No one's hurt you, have they?" His gaze drifted to the right, Jericho's way.

She shook her head. "No, not like that. Someone's been playing mean tricks the last few weeks. And I have proof that Rider Longley's the one doing it."

His eyebrows knit together. "Why does that last name sound familiar?"

"Someone in his family is suing Dad's company. His parents were the ones who died in the crash.... He hates me."

Tripp's mouth pulled into a sneer. "And he's *here?* You let him work on your property? Oh, Alison. This is all worse than I thought."

She bunched up her hands, her nails digging at her palms. "I didn't know before, but I'm going to fire him. Right now. I think it'd be better if you came with me. I don't know what he's capable of."

Tripp gave a wide smile. "Of course. I'm really happy that you asked me. That you trust me. Let's do it now."

She nodded, and he took her hand. Jericho called out her name, sounding wary, but Ali waved him off as she climbed into her truck. At a jaw-rattling speed, she drove to the upper heifer field where they found Rider checking the new calves.

"Need something, Miss Ali?" The lanky cowboy looped his hands around his belt buckle as she and Tripp walked toward him.

"Yes, actually, I do. You're fired. Leave my property and never return."

Rider staggered backward, his shoulders sagging like she'd delivered a physical blow. "But why? I know I'm still learning."

"How can you stand there and pretend you haven't done anything? Did you think that little prank to my tires was funny? How many of my cows have died because of your *unfortunate* fence clipping?" She brushed off Tripp's restraining hand and advanced toward Rider, challenging him.

Rider's eyebrows climbed above the brim of his hat. "I'm trying to catch that person. Ma'am, I'm willing to sleep out here and—"

"Oh, that's rich. Sleep out here so you can successfully set my house on fire? Was that your little plan last night?"

"A fire?"

"Cut the puppy-dog sad-eye act. Your family is suing me. Do you deny that?"

"Well, no, but—"

"Right. So get off my property before I give you a real reason to sue me."

"Miss Ali, I—"

Tripp stepped in between the pair, blocking Ali. He crossed his arms. "I believe the lady's said her peace. If I were you, I'd get on out of here without another word. Remember, I'm a lawyer, and I'll make sure any words you say now come into the courtroom should this escalate."

Giving one stiff nod, Rider turned and barged toward his red truck. Relief rushed through her veins, and for a moment it felt like the world was right again. But then she remembered the sabotaged wagon.

"What am I going to do?"

Tripp snaked his arm around her shoulders, turning her toward him. "About what?"

"The wagon we use for events, you know, the hay cart? Rider sawed through the axle. We have a couple hundred people coming here tomorrow, and nothing besides food booths. I promised a ride to donors." She covered her face with her hands. "The entire fundraiser is going to be a failure."

"Leave everything for tomorrow to me."

The morning of the "Dream A Little Dream" event rolled in with a cloudless sky and an over-enthusiastic sun. But despite the heat, Ali flittered from group to group with a giant smile plastered on her face. Really, her cheeks had started to hurt.

The makeshift parking lot—a plowed-over field on the east side of the ranch—couldn't cram in another car. The tantalizing, sweet smell of kettle corn saturated the air, almost covering the equally enticing burgers sizzling on the giant grill. People mingled together in small groups scattered across the lawn. Some stood near the therapy horses, which were latched to posts on the corral, looking their finest with braided manes and ribbons tied to their tails. All thanks to the Big Sky Dreams students who had showed up early to decorate. The horses stomped from time to time, flicking away flies. Attendees petted their noses and took their pictures. A demonstration, complete with students of all riding levels, would close the event in the next hour.

The hum of a local band performing on the front porch drew a ready crowd. Some of her students clapped out of rhythm, but no one seemed to mind. Most of all, people who didn't even know Big Sky Dreams existed showed up because they spotted the hot air balloons floating above the ranch.

All thanks to Tripp Phillips.

"Ready for an adventure? You promised to go up with me." The very man reached out his hand to her and led her to the front of the balloon ride line. Tethering ropes tied to the baskets allowed them to be hoisted up and down, giving each paying group a ten-minute ride into the skies. Well, more of a hover than a ride. The tethered balloon only rose a hundred yards or so over the ancestral ranch house, but guests still filled the queue, tittering with excitement all the same.

She bit her lip and peeked over her shoulder to try to spot Jericho in the crowd. "You sure these things are safe?"

Tripp grinned, tugging her into the wobbling wicker basket. She yelped when the balloon pilot turned the level on the fuel tank, enabling three-foot flames to dance within the rainbow-themed balloon. She worried her hair might catch fire. With a jolt, they started to rise. Ali stumbled back against Tripp, laughing. He wrapped an arm around her waist.

"Thank you." She turned to Tripp, who watched her and not the scenery. "This is amazing. I don't know how you worked it out in one night, but thank you for making this happen."

His lips spread into an easy smile. "I had some favors to call in. I'm happy to help you." His expression changed. "Chance tells me you're going camping this weekend?"

The wind whipped hair across her face, and she brushed it away. "He's pretty set on it."

"I don't want you to go. It's not safe. Not if Jericho is going. I can't understand why you'd leave him alone with your son, either."

"Well, I can't go back on my word now. Chance'll freak."

"Who cares what he thinks? He doesn't need to get what he wants all the time. You're the parent. Act like it."

"Excuse me?" Ali narrowed her eyes.

Tripp took her gently by her upper arms. "I'm sorry. That

came out wrong. I just don't like the idea of you and that man out there alone together. Don't I have the right to voice that?"

She pulled away. The basket swayed. "We won't be alone. Chance—the whole reason we're going camping—will be there." Turning her back to Tripp, she bumped into a fuel tank, stubbing her toe against the hard metal. "Ouch! Okay, that's it. I'm ready to go back to earth now."

With a fire in his belly, larger than the one shooting from the burners on the balloons, Jericho waited for Ali's ride to finish. He forced his clenched fists to open. Punching Tripp Phillips, as pleasant as it might be, couldn't happen. Not in front of a crowd. Not while Ali thought he hung the moon for orchestrating this event overnight.

A thought kept coming back, like a mosquito in a closed room. It didn't seem possible for Tripp to have planned all this in one evening. If the man had known that Ali's wagon would be sawed through and had worked out the balloons and band weeks ago...now that made more sense.

When their basket touched down, Ali exploded out of the doorway, and Jericho strode forward to meet her. He warred with himself for a moment. Should he tell her about the phone call and the horrible news right before the riding demonstration? The set of her brows told him to wait.

Clamping his mouth shut, he walked beside her. While she stomped her boots and gave orders, he helped the students mount the horses. Jericho quieted the crowd with a shrill whistle, then handed a microphone to Ali.

"Welcome to our first annual 'Dream A Little Dream' event. Is everyone having a good time?"

A round of applause and a smattering of cheers erupted. Jericho unlatched the corral, parading the first horse and rider into the arena by a lead rope while Ali explained the methods used for therapy riding. After three students demonstrated more advanced techniques, the last kid, astride Chief, performed a very slow barrel race.

"Well done, Ned! I don't think I want to try racing against you anytime soon. You'd give me a run for the winner's purse for sure." Her voice sung through the speakers, and the crowd chuckled good-naturedly. As she closed up the event, thanking everyone and giving special recognition to the companies volunteering time and supplies, the crowd clapped, then began to disperse with a rumble of chatter.

Later in the evening, after picking up the trash littering the ranch and unbraiding horse hair, he had a chance to inch up next to Ali again. "I think everything went well. What do you think?"

Hair limp from sweating all day, Ali tipped her face his way as they walked toward the house. Her nose and cheeks were red from being sun-kissed, and the caramel coloring in her eyes glowed in the fading sunlight.

So cute.

"It did go well. I don't know the money count, but I have to believe we raised enough to get us over the latest hump. Beyond that, it was just exciting to see so many people learn about therapeutic riding for the first time. If anything, we opened up some eyes to a need."

Jericho decided to start in on his news in a slow, deliberate way. "It was a wonder. Tripp sure has a lot of connections around town. Powerful connections. I feel like, after seeing this today, that man could get his hands on just about anything he wanted."

"Tripp saved us. Without him, there wouldn't have been an event today. Even if we still had the wagon, it would have been Podunk at best."

Catching her arm, Jericho brought her up short before the porch steps. "I think he's dangerous."

"Dangerous? Funny—he said the same about you." Her eyes narrowed.

"I don't know how to say this kindly, but I got a call today from the vet." Jericho looked up into the purple-dusted evening sky, wishing he didn't have to tell her. "He gave me the findings on Denny, because I paid for the necropsy. Ali, Den was poisoned."

"Po-poisoned?" Ali's knees buckled.

Jericho lurched forward, catching her by the elbows. "Yeah. Not by eating the wrong plants, either. The doctor said it was some pretty strong stuff called Ricin. He was amazed that anyone besides a medical researcher would have access to it. Guess the stuff's been used in warfare to kill people before." Sliding down, he helped her sit on the porch steps.

She pulled away, her head in her hands. "Someone did it on purpose? Killed Denny? Why?" Her voice caught.

Jericho wrapped an arm around her shoulder and pulled her against his side. "Yes. I'm so sorry. Someone killed him— someone who's around this ranch from time to time, who has the kind of pull around town to get his hands on strong experimental medicine."

Chapter Seventeen

Ali scanned the Blodgett Canyon, pulled in by its beauty. Even after a last-minute attempt to beg off joining the boys on the camping trip, one look up the wooded trail told her a hike would slough away her worries more effectively than staying at home would have. At least Kate wasn't home alone; thankfully Megan had volunteered to stay with her.

"I'm just saying, this doesn't seem like enough stuff." Jericho pulled the last of the three backpacks from the truck bed, looping the largest over his shoulders.

"You're the one who told me not to pack any dinner." She bent, adjusting the itchy string of bells Jericho had forced her and Chance to tie around their ankles before exiting the truck. "Seriously, these bells are overkill."

Chance danced around, jingling like a Christmas elf.

Jericho grinned. "They'll ward off wildlife. You know that. Lions and bears."

"And tigers, oh, my." Ali stood and adjusted the straps to her backpack.

With a laugh, Jericho tilted his head toward the mountains. "No tigers in these parts that I'm aware of, but plenty of other dangerous critters."

"Right, with all the rabid carnivores we'll encounter on our hike in broad daylight." She rolled her eyes.

"When the huckleberries ripen late like they did this year, we could run into a black bear or two. Why take the risk?"

Chance grabbed a bag from Jericho's grasp. "But they're scratchy."

Jericho tweaked Chance's nose. "Then you, my boy, should have worn longer socks."

Ali took the bundle out of Chance's hands. "I still think you should have let me pack more food."

Jericho's eyes widened. "Are you kidding? Why lug a bunch of weight when the streams are bursting with rainbow trout?"

"I don't know how to fish." Chance latched on to Jericho's hand with his cast-free one.

He patted her son's head before adjusting his pack. "That's because I know your mom is secretly afraid of fish. She won't even swim in a lake because she thinks they might bite her."

Chance giggled.

"You know I can hear you, right?" Ali pushed back her hair, a line of perspiration already dribbling down her back.

Jericho winked at her over his shoulder. "You just stick by me, Chance. I spent most of my weekends growing up in these mountains."

She kicked a small rock on the path, and it rocketed into the field. "It wasn't that they would bite me. I don't like when they get too friendly and rub their slimy fish bodies against me."

"And how many times have you had that happen to you?" At least he had the decency to hide his wicked smirk behind his hand.

"Lake Como. You were there. Once was enough."

The tall grasses surrounding the entrance to the path popped with the color of wildflowers. The buzz of bees filled the air. Following Chance's excited but inexperienced pace, they completed the short stint through the densely packed forest on the trail. The damage from the great fire, more than ten years ago, still showed dominance with charred trees, many felled, poking out through the glasslike surface of Blodgett Creek. She remembered the terror of the days the fire ripped across the Bitterroot Range, flames licking the night sky and making national news. Such destruction, and it still had a deep hold on this land. Yet new growth flourished, green sprouting out among the ashes.

The resilience of the mountains made her wonder if she too could rise through the ruins, or if that kind of rebirth remained reserved for nature alone.

Her eyes trailed over to Jericho. Did he remember she used to think the jeans and crisp, white T-shirt he donned was the most attractive outfit any man could wear? With two days' worth of soft cocoa-colored stubble on his jaw, he *knew* that drove her crazy in a good way. *Aggravating man.*

Midway through the climb, as the creek narrowed, the trail became talus with large, loose, shaky rocks.

Ali wobbled on a ledge. "This is getting steep quicker than I remember."

Jericho reached out to steady her, taking her hand to guide her over a treacherous lean of boulders. "Want me to carry your pack for you?"

She shook her head.

Chance puffed beside them, hands on his knees. His face flushed. "You can carry my stuff."

Jericho patted his head. "Naw, you're strong. If I remember right, there's a waterfall just up the bend here that we can rest by."

Chance pouted. "I don't think I like hiking anymore."

Jericho laughed. "Here. I'll take your bag, but then I need you to keep an eye out for any little sticks you see because we'll have to find some kindling along the way. Does that sound fair?"

Chance's shoulders slumped. "How big do the sticks have to be?"

Jericho held his thumb and pointer finger a couple inches apart. "Just like this. Not big at all. We won't have a fire for dinner tonight without kindling. See, it's sometimes the really small stuff that's the most important."

Chance jabbed a finger into his own chest. "Like me? I'm small."

Jericho squeezed his shoulders. "Like you. You're really important to both of us. We wouldn't be camping if you hadn't wanted to go, right?"

Chance looked up for a moment, shielding his eyes with his casted arm. "Okay. So how long until the waterfall?"

"Five, maybe ten more minutes." Jericho shrugged.

When Chance bounded ahead, Jericho tried to stand, but stumbled a little. He winced. Ali caught his arm. He used her as leverage to get to his feet.

"Is your leg hurt?"

He smiled. "No more than usual."

They trudged side by side until a cool mist settled on Ali's hair. "Wait. There really is a waterfall?"

"'Course. Why would I lie to him?"

"I don't know. To get him off your back. To stop him from asking questions. People give kids false promises all the time."

"Not me."

Chance jogged back. "Hey, Mom. There's a stream. Can I go in the stream?"

"Let's make sure your bells are tight." Jericho leaned over and adjusted his bells, which proved a difficult task with Chance wiggling so much. When the boy's bells were secure, Jericho turned and grabbed Ali's foot. "Let's make sure your string's on good, too."

She set her foot on his thigh while he adjusted her bells.

"Wow, thanks. Sure wouldn't want those beauties to go any-where."

He stood. He shook his head at her, but the crinkles around his eyes betrayed that he fought a smile. "While we're at it, my little sass-mouth, let's make sure everyone drinks a lot of water when we're resting."

As the afternoon sun baked the backs of their necks, the troop struggled up the long, steep pitch. Jericho continued to encourage them along and asked often if Ali or Chance needed anything. When the sun began its plunge into the western sky, Jericho deemed a small piece of land where the rock met the forest the ideal spot for camping.

"Watch those cliffs for mountain lions, okay buddy? That's your job right now."

"And if I see one, jingle my bells, right?" With his back to Jericho, Chance kept his gaze on the granite cliffs.

Pulling the three-man tent from her bag, Ali hid her grin. The probability of a lion waltzing around on the craggy can-yon walls before nightfall rivaled that of an African elephant plodding up to their campsite and asking for a cup of tea. After dusk could be a different story, but then a roaring fire in the rock pit that Jericho constructed would keep animals away.

Jericho took the tent from her and limped over to the small clearing. As he pulled out the wrapped canvas, his brows drew together. "This thing's as thin as a fly's wing."

"It's ancient. That's Dad's old tent. I had to dig around in the maintenance barn to find it."

"Where's the ground sheet?"

She set aside the frying pan and mugs. "I didn't bring one."

"I don't see a rain tarp in here, either."

"It's pretty sunny."

He stood. His mouth pulled into a grim line as he rubbed his forehead. "You didn't bring one? The weather changes here every ten minutes. C'mon, Ali."

His tone propelled her to her feet. "*You* said pack light!"

Hands tossed in the air, he rolled his eyes. "That doesn't mean don't bring essentials. What are we going to do if those clouds let loose? There isn't shelter for miles." He thrust a hand toward the ominous sky cover rolling across the mountains.

Ali gulped. "It'll miss us." Feigning nonchalance, she resumed unpacking her bag.

"Sure hope so, or else we're all gonna get a good soaking."

"Oh, drop it already and put up the tent. Or put it aside and I'll take care of it."

Leaving his mountain lion patrol post, Chance joined them, with a pink bitterroot flower that looked a little like a water lily cupped in his hand. "You two sound just like Mark's parents."

Heat spread up her neck. Ali pretended not to hear.

"That blush looks good on you, Ali." The tease thickened Jericho's voice. He went about setting up the small tent, a task that took him a total of six minutes. Chance offered unneeded instruction, but said he couldn't help because of his cast.

"You know the story behind that flower you're holding?" Jericho asked Chance.

"Yes. The mountains are named because there are lots of these."

"Well, there's more to it than that. Why don't you ask your mom to tell you the story? Then you and I can go catch some dinner."

"Mom? Do you know why this is called a bitterroot?" Chance crossed their makeshift campsite and plunked the flower into her hands.

Ali cradled the deep pink petals against her palm. They were too beautiful for such a terrible name.

"If I remember right, they were called something else, but then when Lewis and Clark came to explore this area, the

Shoshone Indians cooked up some of the roots and Lewis and Clark spit it out, saying the food tasted bitter to eat."

Jericho joined them and spoke in a low voice. "To the Shoshone Tribe, the bitterroot flowers were a delicacy. They were honoring Lewis and Clark by feeding them the root, but the explorers didn't understand. The Shoshones valued the flowers because they were a source of nourishment, but the same exact thing made Lewis and Clark gag. Kind of interesting how people can experience the same thing and yet view the outcome so differently."

As the sun dipped below the horizon, they spent the waning hours around the fire. The smell of cooked fish permeated the air as Jericho told stories that had Chance giggling until bedtime.

The evening air, spiced with the sweet hint of paintbrush flowers and blue beardtongue, drifted over where Jericho lay. The trace of a fresh rain smell worried him. He bunched an arm under his head like a pillow. A night spent on the hard-packed ground would cause him pain tomorrow, but Ali wouldn't welcome him in the tent. When the first couple drops of rain hit his face, he didn't have much of a choice.

Crawling, he bit back a howl as his left knee wrenched the wrong way. The hike up proved more difficult than he'd realized. Jericho sighed. What else in his life would he have to eventually give up because of his injury?

The zipper on the tent stuck, and he had to play with it a moment before scooting inside. He fumbled in the absence of starlight, but a quick perusal showed Ali lying on the left side with Chance in the middle. Jericho shuffled to the boy's other side.

"What are you doing?" Ali's voice came out as a demanding whisper.

"It's raining outside."

Ali took a loud, deep breath. She rolled onto her other

side, her nose probably touching the tent wall. Jericho gently moved Chance over a bit, then edged into the foot of space along the canvas wall. The light pitter-patter of rain sprinkled against the sides.

Ali's hushed voice jolted his eyes open a moment later. "'Fess up."

"Come again?"

"What's wrong with your legs? You've been limping like a cowboy straight off a cattle drive all day. Tell me straight, or sleep outside."

Licking his lips, he considered a lie. But at some point she would have to know the truth, and a lie now would only make things worse. "I got hurt while stationed overseas." It was easier confessing it quietly into the darkness of the tent than having to look at her.

"Got hurt?" Her voice went up a notch.

"I was on a mission, and we heard someone calling for help in a building. So I went in with some of the guys from the unit. As we searched the third level, a suicide bomber ran into the ground level."

"Oh, no."

"We had seconds before the place exploded. It happened so quickly. I lit for one of the windows and jumped to the ground. Landed on my feet and ran to safety. Shouldn't have been able to do it. Guess it was the adrenaline and all. We lost the rest of the guys in the blast." He paused, choking back the emotions that surfaced every time he thought about his dead friends.

Silence hung between them.

"But you…you weren't hurt?" Her voice cracked.

"God only knows how I got back to base. I reported what happened. But then the pain hit me, made me double over. I collapsed and woke up the next day in a dusty army hospital, both of my knees swollen to the size of basketballs."

"Broken?"

"No, just ruined for good."

"What exactly does that mean? For good?"

He shrugged. "Means I'm not what I once was. I'll have to have knee replacements on both legs before long. And even after that, my legs will never be what they once were."

"Then you're not *ever* going back?"

"No. My army career ended that day, and as I realized that while lying in the hospital bed, I almost gave up. They thought they'd lose me to pure dehydration and depression because I wouldn't touch anything. I nearly died during recovery. But the one thing that kept me going—the single thought that gave me any hope—was you."

The pitter-patter of rain became a rattling, full-out bucket-toss against the tent.

He exhaled. "I had all this time to think over everything that had happened between us. I just wanted to come home and be with you. Each night I dreamed, picturing you running to me when you saw me for the first time. Wishful thinking." He chuckled.

She snorted. "Instead I ran away from you. Sorry about that."

"You gave an honest reaction. I see now, more than ever, how much I deserved your censure. What kind of creep walks out on his wife?"

"Jericho—"

His voice hardened. "If you let me, I promise I'll spend the rest of my life making it up to you."

"I'm just sorry. Sorry you had to go through all that to become the man you are now. I'm sorry I wasn't enough, as your wife, to help you through everything." Her voice caught, and in the closed-in area he could sense her shoulders shaking with tears. He reached out, draping his arm over Chance, who moved a bit. His little feet dug into Jericho's side. Jericho shifted, then ran his hand up and down Ali's exposed arm.

"Shhh. Don't say that, honey. You were everything I

needed, and I was too blind and lost to know it. You were faithful and marched around my walls, trying to tear them down, trying to get inside to reach me. But just like my namesake, I was too stubborn. It took a lot of horrible things to make my walls crumble from the inside out. It was the only way."

"I forgive you." He barely heard her muffled words. Heart jackhammering against his chest, Jericho squeezed her arm, then left his hand lying on her shoulder as he fell asleep.

"Nooooo!"

A frightening wail woke him. Jericho bolted up, smacking his head against the low side of the tent and sending a rush of water through the canvas in the process.

"Mom-maa-aaa-aa!" Chance lurched as a crash of thunder shook the ground.

Jericho's skin prickled. He scooped up the boy and rocked him against his chest as Ali sat up, looking at Jericho with wide eyes.

"Hey buddy, we're here." She pushed out of her sleeping bag and laid a hand on the child's arm.

Chance twisted away from Jericho, wrapping his arms around his mother's neck.

The cracks of lightning made it possible for Jericho to assess their damages. Water flooded the bottom of the tent, and the triangular top threatened to cave under the sag of water at any moment. The trees surrounding the area made their campground unsafe to ride out a storm. They couldn't stay here.

A rumble shook more rain onto them.

"We're going to die! I hate camping. We're all going to die!" Chance sobbed into Ali's neck as she ran her hands over his hair, trying to soothe him. Jericho felt helpless to deal with the howling boy, but he could go find them a safer location. He inched toward the door. Chance's small hand sprang out and stopped him.

"Don't go. Don't leave us here alone."

Jericho's heart poured out with love for him. Everything inside him wanted to go and take both his wife and her son in his arms. He wanted to form a shelter around them that nothing could break apart. Meeting Ali's eyes, his heart seized, because written there he found Chance's same plea: *Don't leave us.*

Crawling back to his loved ones, Jericho worked the watch off his wrist and pushed it into Chance's hands. "My dad gave me this watch, and my grandpa gave it to him. I'm giving it to you to hold for me. That's how you know I'm coming back. Okay, buddy? All I'm going to do is find somewhere safer for us and then come back for both of you."

Biting down on her lip, Ali nodded.

"But I dooooon't want you to goo-oo." Chance broke into a fresh torrent of tears. The tent drooped lower under the weight of gathering water.

"Chance. Hey, I need you to be extra brave for me. Your mom needs a guy to protect her while I'm gone. Can I trust you to do that?"

Sniffling, Chance gave one little nod. Jericho turned to leave, then went back to Ali. He cupped the side of her face, and she leaned into his hand. "I *will* come back for you guys."

Sloshing out of the campsite, Jericho lost his balance and grabbed for a nearby tree. Missing it, he went down hard into the gathering mud. As he rose, a ball of pain scorched his knee. His muscles screamed at him to crumble to the ground again, to weep against the ache. But *they needed him.*

That thought pressed him forward through the torrential downpour into the canyon.

The minute Jericho slipped out of the tent, doubts assaulted Ali's mind and dared to yank away any hope rooted by their earlier whispered conversation.

No more army. No more leaving.

As she leaned her chin on Chance's head, her husband's words danced through her mind. *I just wanted to come home. The single thought that gave me any hope was you. If you let me, I promise I'll spend the rest of my life making it up to you.*

Her poor Jericho. All he had been through in the past eight years wrenched at her heart. The same experience might have produced an angry and bitter man in someone else. Instead he had grown compassionate, patient and confident.

And he had *nearly died*. That halted her thoughts. In all the years of his absence, the fact that he could die never really occurred to her. Goose bumps rose along her arms—whether from the chill of the rain pouring into the tent, from Chance's quiet sobs, or from the thought of losing Jericho, she couldn't be certain. She did know that she never wanted to feel this way again. Raw from eight years of bitterness. Could offering forgiveness really heal her, too?

Pop. Pop. Pop.

The top of the tent began to shudder, ripping from aged seam to aged seam under the weight of the water pooling at the top. Chance screamed as a trough full of rainwater gushed down, drenching them. Shivering in the huddle of torn canvas, Ali peeked at the storm. The violence of the striking lightning shook the small cliff face they camped on. She prayed the forest wasn't dry enough to ignite like it had ten years ago. A powerful wash of rain sent their pots and pans crashing and clanging over the edge of the mountain. A scream lodged in her throat, Ali yanked Chance out of the way.

She worked her lip and brushed the damp hair from her face as she cradled Chance tighter against her. Should they get up and leave? Seek shelter on their own? Something might have happened to Jericho. He had bad knees, after all. Ali shouldn't have let him go out onto the slippery mountainside.

"Chance! Ali!" The man's voice boomed through the forest. His call thawed out her nerves, and with shaking legs she pulled Chance to his feet.

"Over here, Jericho!" she hollered.

Lightning sliced the night sky, eliminating the outline of Ali's protector, his white T-shirt clinging to ready muscles. He slogged toward them, and she could tell from the set of his brow what all the climbing today cost him.

"You came back." She breathed as he drew near.

"Always, Ali." He crouched down, scooping Chance into his arms. "Follow me." He pressed his lips close to her ear so she could hear him over the howling wind. "I found a place that'll keep us safe."

Chapter Eighteen

The rush of rainwater formed a thick rut along the mountain path as Ali ducked her head, trying to follow Jericho's steps while he carried Chance. Wind whipped over her, threatening to toss her off the cliff's edge. Rain plastered her hair and stole her sight. Blinking, she slipped, her legs splaying out at awkward angles in the mud as a shriek caught in her throat. Tumbling forward, her foot caught, and she slammed down onto her chin. A warm metallic taste registered on her lips. *Blood.* Pressing up onto her knees, she wiped her mouth and bit back tears. She couldn't see them anymore. Gone.

"Hey. There you are." Jericho appeared through the tree line, Chance clinging to him like a burr. "You hurt?"

She shook her head. "I'll live."

He bent and offered his hand. Knees wobbling, she rose. He laced his fingers through hers and led them to a natural stone staircase. They splattered up and tripped on the slicked rocks a time or two before reaching the top of the climb. The scent of decaying leaves and wet moss clung to her nostrils.

"Almost there," he said.

Jericho hesitated, but when a flash of lightning lit the sky, he jerked to the left and tugged Ali along. Traversing over a mound of jumbled rocks, he motioned to a small chasm in the mountain wall. Not quite deep enough to be called a cave, an overhang blocked the small area from the worst of the storm's wrath.

Stooping, he shuffled into the den and dropped down. "We're safe now, bud."

"I want my bed. I hate camping." Chance stomped his little foot.

"It's not so bad. You'll have an adventure to tell Kate and Megan about, won't you?"

Chance stuck out his bottom lip. "I'm not ever doing this again."

"Come here, Chance." Her son needed no more invitation to climb into Jericho's lap.

Scooting onto the dry earth, Ali leaned her head against the rock wall. They were closed in tight. Leaving a foot of space between herself and the boys meant half her body still got a sprinkling of rain from the unprotected opening.

Jericho lifted his arm, making room for her. "Come here. I promise I won't bite."

Running a hand over her drenched hair, she gave him a wary look then slid over a fraction of an inch. He leaned over, hooked her by the waist and pulled her against his side. She shouldn't be this near to him. His presence, even waterlogged and cold, had the power to throw her off course. But did that even matter anymore? Not tonight. Not when it felt like they were a hundred miles from another person. Not with her family tucked tightly together. For the first time since Denny's death, warmth spread through her body, almost alleviating the ache inside.

Chance motioned to her. "Come closer, Mom."

Kate's words replayed in her head. *Your family wants you. Why would you say no to that?*

Pressing herself along Jericho's side, she reached out to her son. Chance looped his arms around her neck and pressed his downy cheeks against her neck. The bottom half of his body draped across Jericho.

"I love you, Mom," he whispered.

Words caught in her throat. "You too, Chance."

"And you, Jericho," Chance mumbled against her hair.

Jericho tightened the hold he had on Ali's shoulder, his heart doing a double-time march.

He wound his free arm over Chance's legs and swallowed against the gritty lump in his throat. "Hey, love you too, bud."

As the child's breathing evened, Jericho shifted to look at Ali. His stomach catapulted into his throat. Turned to the side, her face was only inches from his. It would take a mere second to lean forward and brush his lips against hers, to test her response. But Ali's eyes searched his with such intensity that he looked away. He could tell by the tilt of her head that she considered telling him the truth.

He's my son. Isn't he? The words almost reached his lips, but he reined them in. He could never be satisfied without his wife and her son in his life. His insides seared like hot metal. He wanted it all. But he'd forfeited all those privileges eight years ago.

He didn't even know what to do when the child cried. Weeks ago, Ali had been right to say that Chance had only one parent, her. Jericho sure didn't know how to take care of Chance. It wasn't like he had had a stellar example of a father.

But I am. The words from his memory flooded his heart.

Jericho squinted out into the storm. *God?* The voice sounded so real. So he silently prayed, asking God to protect his family as they rode out the storm, and that their return hike tomorrow would prove uneventful.

"Tripp wants to marry me."

Her words jarred him worse than a slap upside the head. He swung around, trying not to disturb Chance. "What?"

She brushed the hair from Chance's forehead.

His lips tightened. "You can't. We're married. You can't." Not his most convincing or eloquent argument, but it's all he had.

Leaning the side of her head on Chance's, she locked gazes with Jericho. "I don't know anymore. I don't know anything."

"Are you in love with him?" He hated his sudden shortness of breath.

Lifting her head, Ali offered a tight-lipped smile. "He's been very good to us."

"But—"

"He's handled all the stuff with the lawsuit. Then, even though it's not in his realm of practice, he found answers to all my other questions about setting up Big Sky Dreams, and he found someone at the firm he works at to go over all the paperwork when Ma got admitted to the home. Then when your dad had his stroke, Tripp seemed just as upset about it as anyone, and he came to tell me first."

"That doesn't make any sense. He's always hated me and Pop." Jericho tried to keep the growl out of his voice.

"Maybe hate's not the right word." She looked up and to the left, one eye squinting a bit in thought. "Jealous? That fits better. I think, for some reason, he was always jealous of you. I mean, look at it. From the outside, all he knew was that you grew up the son of a rich rancher, while he had a single mom who struggled to make ends meet. Maybe, I don't know, maybe that's why I have a soft spot for him— the single-mom part."

Jericho didn't like talking about soft spots in her heart, not if they had anything to do with Tripp Phillips. "No. I think it's just that he's always been smitten with you and now he thinks he has his chance to move in for the kill."

She looked out at the steady cascade of water flowing down the rocks.

He jerked his bum knee to the side. "I don't want you around him. He's dangerous."

She turned, and her eyes flashed. "I'm grateful to you for watching over us these last few weeks. But you can't tell me who I can and can't spend time with."

He gritted his teeth together. Technically, he could do exactly that. "I think he's behind the stuff that's going on at the ranch."

Ali shook her head. "No. You're wrong. It was Rider. I fired him. Nothing's happened since."

"Nothing's happened in two days. So that means you're in the clear?" He cocked an eyebrow.

"Maybe."

"Let me tell you what I think. Tripp Phillips has always been sweet on you, and none of this started happening until I came back in town. If Rider Longley had some vendetta against you, don't you think he would've done something about it sooner?"

Her brow formed a V. The patter of rain began to lessen, signaling the end of the storm.

"Connect the dots. We know for sure that Tripp saw us together at the picnic. You said that he has access to your organization, so that explains the missing money. He knew you'd be at the nursing home the day your tires were slashed. And he's the only person I know with the kind of pull to get his hands on medicine that would down a horse—"

She covered her ears. "Stop!"

"I'm just stating the facts."

Ali blinked a couple times. "Why does everything have to change all the time? Why can't people be as they seem? I hate it."

He adjusted his position, pulling Ali tighter against him. "Not all change has to be bad."

Her head drooped against his shoulder and she shifted, snuggling into him. "It sure feels that way lately—only bad changes. It's all I've known these last few months. With Ma, and Kate, and you, and Tripp and Den."

Jericho rested his chin on her head. "The stuff that matters doesn't change."

"Like what?" Her breathing began to ease.

"Like God. He's always constant. And Kate might leave, but it won't change the fact that she's your sister and she loves you. One day, when Chance grows up, he'll want to move out of the house, but it won't change the fact that he'll always be your son and he'll always love you."

Jericho stopped and glanced down at her face. Eyes closed, her long lashes splayed out against her sun-kissed cheeks. In sleep, she nuzzled against his chest.

He whispered with the side of his face resting on her head. "And nothing in this world can change the fact that I love you, Ali. I've loved you since we were kids, and I always will. You can tell me to get lost, and I will, but it won't change my love."

Ali cuddled closer to the warmth of the body next to hers. And for a moment she imagined herself home, in her own bed. But the protecting sensation of arms encircling her and the jabs of rocks at her back suddenly brought back last night's escapade.

The golden fire of sunrise crept its way along the granite cliffs when Ali stirred. At some point during the night, they'd slumped down. Jericho lay on his back, and Ali curled like a happy cat beside him. Chance, who'd always been an active sleeper, ended up in the shallow end of the crevasse, his head on Jericho's thigh.

Scooching out from under her husband's arm, she tried not to wake him. On her knees, she looked down at the two males, and a smile tugged at her lips. They looked one and the same—mouths open slightly, hair rumpled, soft expressions on their faces.

Pushing out from under the overhang, she tiptoed down the jumble of rocks and the natural stone stairway. A damp mossy smell flavored the morning air, and from her position, she could see the lake below glittering like a sea of diamonds in the first flood of sunlight.

Their late-night conversation came back to her, and she had to admit that Jericho might be right. Change didn't have to be negative. Each morning ushered in newness, whether the world wanted it or not.

Nothing in this world can change the fact that I love you, Ali.

If only. But the words had been dreamed. Jericho hadn't spoken them. What would she say to that, anyway?

Wandering across the open plane, she chose the path back into the woods. She stopped near their campsite, and her worst fears were confirmed. The tent and most of their belongings had become waterlogged, and a rain-fed river had washed it all into the ravine more than fifty feet below. Good thing they got out while they did, or that could have been them down there. Chance's hatred for camping suddenly sounded entirely rational.

Not ready to return to her sleeping guys, she brushed aside a branch and squished in the mud on a path leading deeper into the woods. The fresh scent of pine engulfed her.

Jericho said God didn't change. But that unsettled her. Because if God didn't change, that meant Ali had been wrong in her anger these past eight years. She'd always pictured God getting upset with her, saying *Enough!* and walking away. And she wouldn't blame Him, either. She'd railed against Him. Spit her rage in His face.

She gasped. "*I* changed. Not you. I walked away."

Ali swiped at the tears on her cheek. Did God hurt as much when she turned and walked away from Him as she had when Jericho left? And yet, He waited with open arms. She felt it. Flipping the image, realizing that she was the one who had left, not God, changed everything in her mind. Her knees felt weak. "I'm so sorry. Forgive me. Please forgive me," she whispered.

When she opened her eyes, her breath caught. Not twenty feet away, a mama moose and her calf grazed on the damp forest grass. They seemed to glide on their stiltlike legs, nosing the ground for tree roots. The sunlight dappled through the canopy, lending a glossy sheen to their black coffee-tinted coats. The cow could charge at her if the mama sensed any threat to her calf, so Ali tried not to move.

But at the sound of a guttural growl, she spun on her heels. Ali found herself face-to-face with a mountain lion crouching on a rocky ledge. In a millisecond she saw that the size of his paw matched the size of her head, and his teeth looked longer than her fingers. Fierce yellow eyes surveyed her, and his muscles coiled beneath a shimmer of golden hair.

Her blood ran cold. *I'm going to die.*

Chapter Nineteen

A chill against his back, Jericho stretched. The pressure of Chance's head resting against his leg made Jericho's lips pull into a smile. His hip burned from digging against the rocks all night, but it seemed like a small price to pay for snuggling with Ali and her son. He groped to the right, his fingers fumbling across rocks. His eyes jolted open.

No Ali.

He sat up, easing a backpack under Chance's head. Jericho crawled to the edge and peered down the path, but found no sign of her. He turned back to her son, and with a growl picked up the bells that should have been tied around her ankle.

He shook Chance's shoulder.

The boy rubbed his mouth. "Whaa?"

"Up, Chance. I need you to wake up and help me."

Chance sat up, blinking his eyes. His brows drew together.

Jericho turned to the side and withdrew the gun from his pocket. He jiggled it, hoping the rain last night hadn't caused any damage. He put it back, then thrust a string of bells into Chance's hands. "Here's the deal. Your ma went for a walk and isn't back yet, so I'm going to go try and find her. I need you to stay here and count to one hundred, then rattle these. Keep doing that until I get back. Okay?"

On his knees, Chance scooted so he could lean against the back wall of the cave.

Jericho squatted beneath the rock overhang. "Now what are you supposed to do?"

Chance yawned. "Count to one hundred, shake this." He jiggled the strand of bells. "Then repeat."

"Good boy. I won't be gone long."

"Why can't I come?"

"What if she comes back while I'm gone? You don't want her to be sad, thinking we left without her, do you?"

Chance shook his head.

"Right. So your job is even more important than mine." He squeezed the boy's ankle and gave a wink as he scrunched backward out of the small cave.

Chance cocked his head. "Are you going hunting while you're gone?"

Jericho raised an eyebrow.

"You have a gun in your pocket. I saw you look at it when you thought I was sleeping."

"Good eyes." He didn't answer the boy's question. No use making him even more scared about his mom. "Start counting."

"One…two…three…do I really hafta?"

"One hundred." Jericho hollered over his shoulder, and Chance resumed his count.

He gritted his teeth. Knee burning with hot fire, Jericho limped down the stone staircase, praying his leg wouldn't give out altogether and send him tumbling over the edge.

What was she thinking? Any person with half a mind who lived by the mountains knew that a stroll at dawn meant borrowing trouble. Dawn and dusk were the most active hunting times for the predators here.

He picked up his pace.

Ali was the most incredible woman ever created. Strong and independent, but willing to accept help, she let a man feel like she needed him. Beautiful, even when drenched to the bone. Laughing and open often, but guarded when necessary. He didn't understand what was happening between them, but the last few days felt different. Ali seemed to trust him more. Confusion reigned sovereign in the stampede of emotions, but he'd take whatever she wanted to offer.

Nothing remained of the original campsite. The tent and all the belongings they'd left last night had tumbled down the side of the cliff. His stomach lurched. That could have been them down there at the bottom of the ravine. A prickle ran up his neck. Where could she be? He inched toward the edge of the cliff. She wouldn't try to free-climb to their stuff, would she? Nothing down there was worth risking her neck for.

A throaty cat cry ripped the still air.

Ali? Please, God, no!

With strength born out of terror, he sprinted toward the source of the sound, yanking the small revolver from his pants pocket as he ran. He swung around a tree, and the sight before him made his blood freeze. Not three feet from Ali, at eye level, a male mountain lion crouched. The animal spit hate in her direction. One swipe of his paw, and she'd be gone.

Aiming the gun into the air, Jericho pulled the trigger, and the crack of the shot resounded against the cliff face. Flinching, the lion dropped back, leaped on a higher rock and scampered away. On the other side of the small clearing, a moose cow and calf took off in a wild charge.

Weak with relief, he dropped the hand holding the gun to his side. On legs wiggly as rubber, he crossed to where Ali stayed rooted, mouth open.

The moment he was at her side, she came unglued. Ali bolted into his arms with a force that almost knocked him over. She burrowed her face into his chest. "He was going to kill me."

Jericho rested his chin on her head, breathing in her sunshine smell. He let his fingers go to the tips of her hair. "Shh. You're fine. You just got in the way of his breakfast is all."

She trembled. "Th-they don't usually go for moose."

"He looked young. Probably still learning. A pretty string of bells would have saved you."

Her hands came up, entwining around his waist as she laid her cheek right over his heart. "I thought he'd kill me. I kept thinking, what would happen to Chance...to you?"

Fear echoed within his racing heart. Every moment with this woman was a gift, and she needed to know it. Jericho licked his lips, relishing the feel of her body melding to his. "I love you. I don't know if you heard when I said it last night. But I love you, Ali. Always have, always will. You know that, right?"

Sniffling, she nodded against him. He placed a kiss on top of her head and left his hand cupped against it.

Despite the morning chill, Ali's entire body blazed. Jericho loved her.

Questions zinged through her mind. Should she say something? Did he only tell her that because she almost died?

As much as the words filled her with longing, they also terrified her. Her life with Chance was so routine. What if it bored Jericho after a time? What if he left again?

Thinking of her son brought her back to reality. A lion had almost ripped off her head. She trembled again. Who would care for Chance if something unexpected happened to her?

She sucked in a breath. "Chance is your son." Had she really just said that?

Jericho went rigid. "What?"

She pushed back from him. "He's yours."

Grabbing her shoulders, his mouth hung slack. "I thought... But... You're certain?"

Ali laughed at his shock. "Of course. You're the only man I've ever been with."

"Did you know? When I left?"

"That's why I stayed up that night. I wanted to tell you, but you came in and—"

He pulled her back into his arms, wetness gathering around his eyes. "I'm sorry. All these years, you were all alone. I'm so sorry, Ali."

She clung to him like a life preserver, needing his strength in that moment just as much as he seemed to need her. "Silly man. I forgave you already."

"He's my son."

"Didn't you already know? You two are mirror images of each other."

"I thought. I hoped." He let go of her, raking a hand over his matted hair. "But hearing it—this is wild." Jericho's hands shook. "What will he say? What if he doesn't want me?"

Joy bubbling up, Ali laughed. "Want you? You're his hero. He already loves you."

"But I'm just flesh and bones. I'll let him down someday. Then what? Maybe we shouldn't tell him. What do I know about being a father?" He paced away, hands in his pockets.

"Jericho. Look at me."

He obeyed.

"You're already the best father he's ever known. Hear me? You're amazing with him. There's nothing to worry about."

They agreed to wait and tell Chance back at home, but the entire climb down the mountain, Ali caught Jericho staring at her. For the past month she'd been so worried about him finding out; now she wondered what took her so long. Ali snuck another glance at Jericho. Hope sung in her heart, but she silenced it quickly. Just because he loved her didn't mean he'd stay forever. He supposedly loved her last time, too.

Ali knocked on Kate's bedroom door.

"Come in."

She pushed inside, and Kate stopped toweling off her hair. "Look at this. Our fearless adventurer back from her travels."

Flopping down on her sister's bed, Ali groaned. "On a scale of one to ten, the camping trip would rank around a two."

"You looked tuckered out when you got home yesterday. I think you set a sleeping record. Was it sixteen hours? Jericho's been here already to collect Chance. He said he had your permission."

Ali sat up quickly, her hand flying to her head. "I did the stupidest thing. Oh, Kate."

"I'm sure you've done stupider."

"No. Seriously. I told Jericho that Chance is his son. Why did I do that?"

"I'm proud of you, Al. You did the right thing."

Ali sprung to her feet. "He scared off the mountain lion, and then I thought about what would happen if I died and I just blurted it out."

"Mountain lion?" Kate met Ali's eyes in the mirror.

"What should I do? I told him he could take Chance for the day. Now it starts, this joint custody stuff Tripp warned me about. At least we live on properties that touch. That'll make everything easier."

"I think you're missing the obvious solution."

Ali jammed her hands onto her hips. "Being?"

"Take Jericho back. Live together. Be a family."

"No. I can't—I'm not ready for that. *He* still terrifies me." Ali hugged her middle.

"Does Chance know?"

She shook her head.

Kate stopped putting on foundation and faced her. "When are you planning on telling him?"

A half laugh, half sob escaped from her lips. "Today."

Her sister jumped up, crossed the room and hugged her. "This is huge."

"We're supposed to tell him tonight, together."

A truck, kicking up a cloud of dust, bumped up the driveway. Ali watched from the window as the delivery man jogged to the back and pulled out a package. Megan trotted from the barn and signed for the box. As the truck pulled away, Megan hurried toward the house. Ali left Kate's room, pounding down the stairs.

"Special delivery!" Megan waved the package.

Ali joined her in the kitchen. "Who's it for?"

"You, sleepyhead." Thrusting the package into her hands, Megan smiled. "Open it."

Pulling at the tape, she pried open the long box. When she peeled back the top, a heady perfume infused the air. She peeked inside and gasped at the colorful bouquet of roses.

She motioned to Megan. "Hold the box for me while I pull these out."

"Oh, they're stunning! Who are they from?" Megan buried her face into the flowers, breathing deeply.

Ali fished out the pink envelope and peeled it open. She read the card out loud. "'Missed you. Waiting for an answer. Tripp.'"

"Here. I'll put these in water for you." Megan grabbed a vase from on top of the fridge and began to fill it at the sink. She looked at Ali over her shoulder. "You know about the stud bull, right?"

Ali pulled a knife out of her pocket, cutting off an inch of the stems. "I know he's ornery as an old schoolteacher."

Megan handed her the vase. "Wait, no one told you?"

"Just say it, Megan." Dropping the flowers into the water, Ali gave them a fluff before placing them on the table.

"He's gone."

Ali cocked an eyebrow. "Define *gone?*"

Megan tossed up her hands. "Vanished. Missing. Snatched." She grabbed the back of a chair. "Did anyone see anything?"

"No. We searched his field. There are no openings in the fence. No sign of tampering."

"Someone can't abduct a two-thousand-pound beast without being seen. I've had enough. I'm calling the cops."

Megan caught her arm before she could get to the phone. "I don't know. Don't you still want to catch Rider in the act?"

"I think it's out of my hands. I thought when I fired him, it would stop."

"I don't like this any more than you do. But let me help you. I'll stick around later the next couple days and try to get some evidence on him. Then we'll have something tangible when we go to the cops. We want them to take us seriously, after all."

Ali rubbed her temples. "Two days. In two days, even if we find nothing, I'm calling the cops."

Chance gave Jericho a toothy grin as they bumped up the driveway.

"So I'm a real cowboy now?"

Jericho winked. "Certifiably."

"Can we tell Mom what I did?"

"Always." He threw the Jeep into Park, and Chance burst out the door and up the porch steps to his mother before Jericho could unbuckle his seat belt.

A smile pulled at his lips as Chance rushed over everything they'd done that day. The kid had his mom by both hands, giving little jerks when something in the story really excited him. When Jericho joined them, Ali looked up and mouthed "thank you."

She propped her hip against the porch railing. "Slow down, sweetheart. You sat on calves? No wonder you look like you haven't bathed in a week."

"Yeah. The ranch hands caught them. Then I'd have to sit on them and hold them real still because Jericho took a knife and castled them—"

"Castrated," Jericho offered.

Chance made a face, and Jericho lifted his hands in surrender.

"The calves didn't like it."

Ali smirked. "I'd imagine not."

"But Mom, you can ask Jericho. I am very strong. He said I had to be to hold the calves down. And I thought they'd hurt me, but I was too tough for them."

Her eyes meandered over Jericho. "That so?"

He squeezed Chance's shoulder. "He turned green for the first fifteen minutes or so, but he held it together. Took a second to find his cowboy grit is all."

"I have it, Mom. Jericho said in spades, which sounds like a lot."

Ali caressed Chance's face. "Sure does. It seems like you had a good time today. Are you starting to like ranching?"

"Yes! Jericho said he'll teach me all the cowboy things that I don't know. They don't use horses for stuff on his ranch. He said I have to go on the dirt bike and ATV before then so I can help. Right?" Chance looked up at him, and Jericho fought wetness in his eyes. His son.

Jericho cleared his throat. "Yep. You'll have to ride with me until you're older, but I'll need you trained by the time I have to sort the herd in the fall."

"Cool. I like spending time with you."

His eyes skittered to Ali's, and she nodded. "Hey, Chance, Jericho and I need to talk to you. It's something very serious, okay?"

Chance spun, grabbing him by the hand. "I'm sorry. I didn't mean to do it."

Mind reeling, Jericho hunched over. "Do what, bud?"

"I broke a tool at your barn today. I pretended to be a knight and used it like a sword, but it got stuck in the tree bark and bent, then I put it back and didn't tell anyone." His small chest heaved.

Dropping into an Adirondack chair, Ali laughed.

Jericho chuckled, too. "I don't care about that. But c'mere." He pulled Chance onto his lap. "Don't ever be afraid to tell me something like that. You can talk to me about anything."

"Okay. Then what do you wanna talk about, 'cause I didn't do anything else wrong today."

Ali took a deep breath, then leaned over and took her son's hand. "Do you remember when you asked about your father?"

Chance nodded. "You said he left because he didn't like you."

Because he didn't like you? Jericho bit down hard on the back of his teeth. Nonsense. He wanted to root that lie right out, but the blush blooming on Ali's cheeks made him hold his tongue. He'd wait till they were alone.

"Yes. But you still want to know who he is, right?"

Chance licked his lips. "Yes. Because even if he doesn't like you, he might like me. Right? Do you think he'll want me?"

Jericho tightened his hold on the boy. "I know so."

"Sweetheart. Jericho is your father."

Chance stiffened in his arms. Jericho's mind whirled. Then his son's little shoulders started to shake, and Chance covered his face.

Jericho stared at Ali, who met his look with wide eyes. "Chance, hey, baby, what's wrong?" She ran her hand over the child's head.

Sucking in his bottom lip, Chance faced Jericho. "You're my dad?"

"Are you disappointed?"

His son sniffled. "No. You're my favorite person in the whole world." He flung his arms around Jericho's neck, choking him.

But Jericho reveled in it, bear-hugging his son back. "I love you, Chance."

"Can I call you Dad?" Chance whispered against his neck.

Jericho swallowed down a lump the size of the Bitterroot Range. "I'd like that a lot."

Ali's eyes swam with tears. She pressed her hand over her mouth as she watched them.

His son pulled back. "Are you going to live here? With us?"

"Well, I'm staying on your couch until we're sure you guys are safe here."

"But you don't want to stay with us forever? Is it because you still don't like Mom?"

Jericho's heart squeezed. He wanted to reassure Ali so badly. He set Chance back so they could make eye contact. "I love your mom."

Springing to the ground, Chance gave a loud whoop. "This is the best day of my life. So you'll live with us and we can be a real family?"

"I'd like that. I'd like that a lot. But that's between your mom and me."

After sending Chance up to take a bath, Ali moved to leave, but Jericho caught her hand. "Sit out here. Watch the stars with me."

He pulled her down onto his lap. He smelled like hard work and country air. He smelled like home.

She tucked her head against his neck. "I think that went well."

Jericho ran his fingers into her hair. "Yep."

A calf in a yonder field bayed as they sat there holding each other. With her eyes closed, Ali listened to the steady thump-thump of Jericho's heart. Her stress was lost in the dependable rhythm.

Tracing his fingers up and down her arm, he broke the silence. "What do you think about what Chance said? About being a family?"

She pushed away from him and stood to grab the railing.

Then she looked out across the mountains. "I'm not ready for anything like that. I can't—"

Jericho came beside her, his shoulder pressing against hers.

"I'm so afraid," she whispered.

"I won't hurt you again, Ali. I promise. I won't leave."

Swiping at her eyes, she turned away from him. But he caught her arm. "Hey, don't run off. We don't have to talk about that right now. I want to be by you is all. We can talk about something else. Anything. Tell me about your day. What did you do with Chance gone?"

Warmth spread through Ali as she stared into his soft eyes. He wanted to be by her. He cared about the mundane happenings in her life. He loved her.

"I had two riding classes. Went to the bank to clean out my mom's safe deposit box—"

He snagged her hand. "Safe deposit box?" Then he laughed. Scooping Ali against him, he spun in a circle. "You're a genius."

He set her down. He fished into his pocket and pulled out a small key. "Pop gave this to me when I first went to visit him. I've been carrying it around all this time wondering what it opened. Go figure. I never thought about a safe deposit box."

"Do you have any idea what your dad would put in it?"

"No, but I'm going to find out tomorrow."

Chapter Twenty

$\sim$

Ali blocked the sun from her eyes as a car maneuvered down the pothole-ridden driveway. She batted at a horsefly.

Chance scampered up beside her. "Is that Dad?"

Ali's heart fluttered. *Dad.* Chance found every opportunity to say the word.

"No, honey. That's Tripp's car."

"Aw, man."

Ali rested her hand on his head. "We like Tripp."

He shrugged. "He's all right."

Before Tripp could climb out of the car, Chance raced to his window and popped his head inside. "Hey, Tripp. Guess what?"

The man slid out of the car and smiled at Ali. "What, Chance?"

"I have a dad."

Tripp's smile disappeared, and his brows plunged. "That so? Well, we all have fathers, but some of us never get to have a relationship with them." He leaned down and tapped his chest. "I had a dad too, but I didn't get to know him or live with him, either. He never claimed me as his. But know what? I had other people in my life instead, like you do."

Chance scrunched up his face. "But I *have* one."

Tripp walked around Chance, briefcase in hand. "Hi, Alison. Hot day. Do you have a moment?"

Chance trailed after him. "My dad is Jericho Freed."

Tripp stopped. "Wh-wh-what did you say, son?"

"Jericho is my dad, and we wrestled down calves together. He took me camping and said I'll like it better next time. And he's living with us now." Chance started to spin.

Tripp's eyebrows arched. "That so, Alison?"

Ali closed her eyes. "He is not *living* here. He's just sleeping on the couch for the time being. Until we know all the threats have stopped."

"Stopped? But you fired Rider?" He raked a hand through his hair, then motioned for her to follow him to the porch. "Why didn't I know about all this?"

Megan stepped out of the barn to wave at them. Chance sprinted over to join her.

At the base of the steps, Ali laid a hand on his forearm. "We'll be okay. Don't worry."

When they reached the porch, he captured her wrist and tugged her into the house. "You told Jericho about Chance? They both know?"

"I couldn't lie anymore. It didn't feel right. Besides, Jericho's a great father. I was cheating Chance out of something special by not telling them." She pulled away from him and crossed to the sink. She started rinsing the plates from breakfast.

"How could you? You have no guarantee he isn't going to pick up and leave again. Now you have a child who's going to be damaged by that. Do you know what it's like to not have a father, then to find out who he is and have him not want you?" Tripp's voice caught, and he turned his back to Ali.

"Tripp?" She wiped her hands on her jeans. Stepping near him, she touched his shoulder.

He took a deep breath. "It'll devastate Chance when Jericho rejects him. He'll leave, and Chance will wonder his whole life what he did wrong to warrant his father's abandonment. And Jericho *will* leave. I can promise you."

"I'm tired of basing my decisions on fear. I had to tell him. What if something happens to me?"

Tripp thumped his chest. "You don't think I would take care of Chance? Didn't I tell you I'd adopt him? I'd be a father to him. But that wasn't good enough for you. *I* wasn't good enough for you, either."

"Oh, no. Tripp, no. It's not like that." She moved toward him, but he stepped back.

"Don't you realize? You've ruined everything. Everything."

With his lips pulled into a snarl, Ali didn't know how to soothe Tripp. Why was he so angry? They both knew he didn't love her. But then what would make him so upset?

"Good morning, Mr. Freed. Are you here about your business?" Miss Galveen, the loan officer, greeted him as he entered the bank.

"No. Everything is set there." Jericho looped his hand around his neck. "Actually, I'd like to look at a safety deposit box, if I could."

The spikes on the heels she wore echoed against the marble floor. "Are you interested in getting a safe deposit box, or do you already have one and need to check it?"

Fishing the key from his pocket, he held it out to her. "If this looks familiar, I need to see this box. If not, I need to figure out which bank uses these keys."

She hovered over his hand. "That's one of ours all right." A single eyebrow quirked. "But you didn't know you had a box? How remarkable, Mr. Freed."

"It's not mine. It's my pop's box, and he gave this to me. He wants me to open it."

"What's the number on there?"

"One thirty-nine."

Miss Galveen crossed her arms. The tight bun on top of her head made her look twenty years older than she was. "I'll have to see if you're authorized." Snatching the key from his hand, she disappeared behind the employee area of the bank.

Jericho rocked on the balls of his feet and resisted the urge to whistle while he waited for her to come back. He dropped down into a leather chair and adjusted his watch.

The click-clack of heels against the floor announced Miss Galveen's return. Using the arms of the chair, he heaved up his body to stand. Working with Chance on the ranch had made his knees numb.

"You may follow me, Mr. Freed. According to the paperwork, you're fully authorized to open this box. I'll take you there now."

He shadowed her across the hall, down a flight of stairs, through some twists and turns and onto the lower level. She pointed at the metal boxes sunken into the wall.

Jericho shuffled forward. "How does this work?"

"I need you to sign this paperwork." She thrust a clipboard and pen at him. "We'll unlock it together, then you may do whatever you want with the contents. When you're done, we'll lock the box together, as well."

After she left, Jericho held the metal container in trembling hands. What could Pop have in here? The latch creaked, and a single piece of paper rested inside. He unfolded it and started to read.

"'This is my Last Will and Testament. I, Abram Freed, being of sound mind and body, leave the entirety of my worldly possessions, my ranch and my wealth to the father of Chance Silver. This Will revokes all prior Wills and Codicils.'"

Jericho's hands shook, and his eyes darted down the page. According to the date, Pop had made the new will a year after Jericho left town. He licked his lips. But then that meant...

"He forgave me. All those years ago." His legs threatened

to collapse. The area lacked a chair, so Jericho wobbled over to the wall and leaned against it. "I should have come home so much sooner."

Dropping his head, he squeezed the bridge of his nose. So many wasted years, while a family waited.

Smoothing out the paper, he scanned the information again. Not that he needed the money or cared about Pop's land. But the gesture of mercy rocked through him. How many times had he told his father he hated him? Hated the Bar F Ranch. But it would be his.

He rubbed his jaw. An emblem at the top drew his attention. *Mahoney and Strong*. That was the firm Tripp worked at. Ali told him that Tripp worked as an associate there.

But then that meant…? His mouth went dry.

Jericho charged up the steps and ran through the bank lobby while Miss Galveen called after him about locking the box. The heavy front doors smacked behind him as he yanked out his keys and roared his Jeep out onto the street.

Swinging into the driveway, his wheels spit gravel. He squinted, trying to identify the car near the house. Tripp's. His grip tightened on the steering wheel. He was surprised his teeth didn't bust at how hard as he clenched them.

Throwing the Jeep into Park, he hopped out and charged toward the house.

Chance appeared, bouncing at his elbow. "Hi, Dad."

He stopped and dropped down to hug his son. "Hey there, buddy. Where's your ma at?"

The boy rolled his eyes. "Inside with Tripp. He's real angry."

Jericho bolted up. "I need to talk to him. Stay out here. Okay, Chance?" He shoved through the front door.

Tripp's voice carried from the kitchen. "Sign it, Alison. It's the only way to keep Chance safe."

"Safe?"

"Freed can't be trusted. Look at his past record. Your troubles didn't start until he got here. I hate even suggesting it, but have you thought that he might be the one causing problems around here?"

"He'd never—"

"He's always been a master at playing you, ever since we were kids. These occurrences have given him ample opportunities to gain your trust. He always seems to be around at precisely the right moment. You don't find that odd?"

Jericho hovered near the kitchen entrance, a tickle running down his spine. Would Ali defend him? Or had he shattered her trust?

Silence. His stomach dropped into the toes of his boots. Wishing he could see her face, he pressed his palm against the door.

Tripp cleared his throat. "Divorce is your only option. He has been nothing but heartache for you your entire life. Cut the dead weight. Choose a new start. Choose me."

Enough. Jericho burst into the kitchen. He bounded toward Tripp and ripped the papers out of his hands. "Like fire that's her only choice!" He whirled toward Ali, shaking the divorce papers in his hand. "Were you gonna sign? Be straight with me."

Her eyes widened. "What are you doing here?"

"Know why he wants you to sign these?" Jericho crumpled the legal documents. "He wants to marry you. And let me guess, he wants to adopt Chance after the wedding. Am I right?"

Tripp and Ali spoke at once.

"Don't answer him, Alison."

"Well, yes."

Jericho's lip pulled up. "'Course I'm right. Know why? Because Tripp here knows about my pop's will. Don't you, Tripp? Found yourself a bit of a loophole. Didn't tell Ali that little tidbit, did ya?"

Ali's gaze ping-ponged from Jericho to Tripp, back to Jericho. "Will someone just spit it out? I don't know what you're talking about."

"He's the one who's been manipulating you. You and Chance are as good as dollar signs in his eyes." Jericho tugged the will from his pocket and shoved it into Ali's hands. She folded back the page, her eyes scanning the paper.

Tripp growled. "How'd you get your hands on that, Freed? That's not public knowledge until your dad's death. How'd you weasel it—did you break into the firm? I could have you arrested."

"My dad's smart enough to secure his own copy."

Ali shook her head. "I don't understand. Why would your dad…?"

Jericho took his wife's hand. "Don't you see? Pop figured Chance was mine. Plus Pop knew, before I even knew, that I'd come back. But Tripp just wanted my dad's money. He doesn't love you, Ali, not like I do."

Tripp made a lurch for the will, but Jericho jerked it away. "I wanted it because your dad's money is rightfully *mine*." His face reddened.

Rocking back, Jericho crossed his arms. "And how do you figure that?"

With a deep breath, Tripp clenched his fists. "Because, as the oldest, I'm the rightful heir. That's how these things work, and Abram just disregarded that, after everything."

Ali squeezed Jericho's arm. "Heir?"

Bracing his hands on the counter, Tripp looked Jericho in the eye. "Meet your older brother."

Jericho's mind spun like a carnival ride. Being plowed over by a charging heifer would have hurt less. "I don't have a brother."

Ali jammed her finger at Tripp. "So it was you all along. You killed Denny, didn't you? You stole money from Big Sky

Dreams. You know what that means to me—to the children. How could you?"

Tripp's eyebrows dove. "Absolutely not! Freed's turning this all around. You can't trust him. How long has he had the will in his possession? How can you be certain he's not the one manipulating you? It seems like quite the coincidence. Funny, he came home when Abram is close to dying, and there is a will naming him sole heir if he wins you back. He simply has to get you to say Chance is his son. When something is that convenient in the courtroom, we call it what it is—guilty."

Jericho crossed his arms to hide his fisted hands before he struck the man. "I'm finding one problem with your logic. There's no motive. I don't need the money, and I could care less about that ranch."

A wicked gleam lit Tripp's eyes. "I heard that you *do* need money. Lots of it, actually. For a little business venture you're doing. Bet he hasn't told you a lick about that, has he, Alison? He told the people at the bank weeks ago he had *a lot of money coming to him*. Interpret that for me."

Ali gasped.

Jericho seized her arms. "Don't listen to him."

"Did you say that to someone at the bank?"

"I did. I have no clue how Tripp would know that. But—"

She yanked out of his grasp. "I want you both out. Now."

"Ali. Let me explain." Jericho took a step toward her.

She stopped him with her palm to his chest. "I don't want to hear it. Get off my property. I don't know who I can trust anymore."

Tripp rounded the counter, but Ali put a hand up to him, as well. "I'm serious. Both of you leave right this second, or I'm calling the cops. You're not welcome on my land."

Jericho snatched the divorce papers from his passenger seat and ripped them until it looked like snow. Would she have signed? It rankled him that she could disregard the entire last month. Like it meant nothing that he'd told her he loved her.

But she'd never returned the words.

His muscles ached like after a hard run. He scratched his head.

Meet your older brother.

Tripp? Jericho did the math—they were what, three months apart in age? Tripp and Jericho had the same build, the same piercing blue eyes. Why hadn't he noticed before?

He stumbled out of the Jeep and into the nursing home. Swirls of over-musked perfume and cafeteria food rushed past as his boots clapped down the familiar hallway. He trudged into his father's room.

Jericho took a deep breath and dropped into the chair beside his dad's bed. "How you doing today, Pop?"

Pop's brow wrinkled halfway.

"Yep. I'm having that kind of day, too. I figured out the key you gave me."

His father pointed at the picture of Chance on his nightstand. Jericho scooped up the photo and ran his thumb over the glass. "You knew all along that I had a son. Why didn't you try to find me?"

Pop grabbed Jericho's knee and gave a gentle squeeze.

"I know. You can't tell me. But Pop, I missed out on seven years. All the time, I had a family waiting."

He took off his hat, placing it on the end of the bed. "I found out something today. I want to check it with you first."

Pop nodded.

The words stuck in his throat. Jericho licked his lips. "I'm just going to spit it out plain." He took a breath and worked his jaw. "Is Tripp Phillips your son?"

Pop bowed his head for a moment. "Yeth."

Lightning rattled through Jericho's chest. "But then, that means you cheated on Mom before she got pregnant with me?"

Pop rubbed his eyebrows. "Yeth."

"Why didn't I know? Why didn't you tell me? I should have *known* I had a brother."

"Ith. Ino. I dondt know."

Jericho closed his eyes. "No wonder Tripp always hated me."

Elbows on his knees, Jericho buried his head in his hands and blew out a long stream of air. Life had been perfect yesterday. How did it go all topsy-turvy in less than twenty-four hours? Feeling the touch of his father's hand on his head, he glanced up. Pop's eyes brimmed with tears, and Jericho's mouth went dry.

He took his dad's hand again. "Don't worry. I'm still here."

Chapter Twenty-One

Ali ached like blood pooling behind a bruise.

She flipped on the faucet, letting cool water trickle to fill her hands. She splashed her cheeks then scrubbed her face on the hand towel, hoping to wash off the blotches and the empty look in her eyes. But a glance in the mirror sent her gripping for the counter.

Scanning her red-rimmed eyes, rumpled hair and drooping mouth, she sucked in a ragged breath. "Pull yourself together, girl."

But this time sapped her more than last. *He's gone.* She'd sent him packing with a threat of the police, and he hadn't loved her enough to stay and fight. *Like last time.* She failed. Failed as a wife when he most needed her to stand beside him, trust him. She knew with bone-deep certainty that Jericho Freed hadn't manipulated her and yet, in the split second that mattered, she'd doubted him.

Ali shoved the towel into her mouth, biting down a sob. Just because she prowled the house at two in the morning didn't mean the rest of the family needed to be woken up.

Would another eight years pass before she saw him again? He could be halfway to Mexico by now. Gone for good.

Without Denny, Ali didn't know what to do with the grief

washing over her. If she could, she'd wander out to his stall
and climb up on his back again. A twilight ride would have
soothed her enough to sleep.

But without him, the pain dared to drown her.

As she tied her robe, a piece of paper taped to the mirror
caught her eye. Kate. One of those three-by-five cards she
loved to scribble on and stick all over the house.

Before, Ali had ignored them, but now she squinted to
read it.

Some trust in chariots and some in horses, but we trust
in the name of the Lord our God.

She snatched it off the mirror, clutching the verse to her
chest. Trust in horses. Jericho had accused her of that. Of
treating Denny like a savior.

"Oh, God. I'm so sorry. I'm not good at trusting You, or
anybody for that matter. I messed up big by not trusting Jericho today. What's going on? I feel so lost. Is it supposed to
hurt like this? I thought freedom would be safe. No more
pain. Aren't You supposed to protect me?"

Stumbling out of the bathroom, she stopped to let her eyes
adjust to the darkness. She crept downstairs.

Her mind meandered like a lost calf, and each thought
cried for attention. Hadn't life been better before Jericho came
back? At least then her emotions had been packed floor to
ceiling with crates labeled Resentment, Bitterness, Anger.
It had been ordered. She had known who she was and what
drove her. But now, after offering forgiveness—after yanking the weeds out of the garden of the soil in her heart—an
empty patch of dirt remained.

On bare toes, she padded across the living room, but she
stopped to trail her hand across the back of the empty couch.
Jericho's couch. She swiped at her cheeks.

Flipping on the kitchen light, she grabbed the tea kettle and filled it with water. Mint tea. That would help her sleep.

Ali smoothed aside her hair and slumped down into a chair.

If only she could think of a way to regain the reins of her life. She sighed. Even before, the control that had been in her grasp had been based on lies. The boy who ruined her life didn't exist anymore. No. Jericho oozed regret. Every action proved him now to be a man of compassion, humility and patience.

Chance needed his father. She couldn't separate them.

She needed her husband.

Ali rubbed her palms against the cool laminate wood on the table.

But the biggest lie had been her own. All these years, she had viewed herself as strong and independent. *Lies.* Ali ran a hand through her hair. She didn't want to be alone. And not just anyone would do. She wanted Jericho Freed.

The kettle rattled with steam.

She poured some water into a mug and leaned her hip against the counter, crossing her arms while the tea steeped. Lurching forward, she spied another of Kate's verse cards taped to the window above the sink. She snatched it and smiled. Like a treasure hunt. What had Jericho called them? Scripture bread crumbs.

"Bread crumbs to lead me home," she mumbled as she shuffled back to the table with the mug and card.

Bear with each other and forgive one another if any of you has a grievance against someone. Forgive as the Lord forgave you. And over all these virtues put on love, which binds them all together in perfect unity.

Perfect unity. She could use some of that.

Kate bumped into the door as she opened it, squinting. "What are you doing up at this hour?"

"Sorry. Did I wake you?"

Kate rubbed her eyes and yawned. "I heard the kettle whistle."

Ali squeezed her hand as Kate took a seat at the table. She rubbed at her eyes and jutted her chin toward Ali's mug. "Do you have any more? It smells good."

Scooting her mug across the table to Kate, Ali got up to pour herself another.

Kate blew away the steam from her tea. "Why are you up?"

"A lot on my mind. I couldn't sleep."

"Are you nervous something bad will happen without Jericho here?"

"No. What if I lost him, Kate?"

Kate slurped her tea. "Huh."

"I love him."

Her sister slapped the table. "Well hallelujah and call it Friday! It's about time you admitted it, even if the rest of us have known for, oh, ten years."

"I think I was afraid. Because owning up to it makes things worse. I think I was safer pretending that I didn't care about him. For that matter, we can lump God in there, too. Depending on Him feels like waiting in a desert for rain."

"But when the rain comes to a desert, it floods with abundance."

"True."

"What are you so confused about, Al?"

She finished the last of her tea but still cupped the mug in her hands, letting the warmth radiate into her chilled nerves. "*Confused* isn't the right word. *Confronted* might be better, or *convicted*."

Kate raised her brows.

"It's your stupid note cards." Ali pushed the two she'd collected across the table. "It's like you planted them special for me tonight. There are little verse booby traps all over the house."

Kate looked over the cards and smirked.

"I've been so stubborn and foolish for *years*. Then I forgave Jericho and told him about Chance. I figured that counted for something."

"It's not like that—"

"I even had this revelation on the camping trip. I did to God what Jericho did to me. I walked away from someone who loved me without looking back."

"That's *huge*, Al."

"But tonight I realized there is something I haven't done. I've never actually surrendered to God. I've never acknowledged that He's in control of my life."

Kate's hand snaked forward and clasped hers. "Do you want to?"

"I'm terrified about what that entails. But yes. Will you pray with me? You're better at this kind of stuff than I am."

She shook her head. "No. I think you need to be the one talking. But I'll hold your hand while you do it."

Ali bowed her head. "I've been in charge of my life for too long and have almost run it into a gully. I'm handing over the reins to You. Amen." She looked at her sister. "Do you think that was okay?"

Kate rubbed her thumb over Ali's knuckle, her eyes shimmering. "I think it was perfect. We're sisters for eternity now."

Ali nodded. "What do I do next?"

"Get to know Him better. Stand firm in His promises."

"His promises?"

"Sure. The Bible's full of them. Like—" Kate popped up and grabbed a card from under a magnet on the fridge "—try this one on for size."

Ali took the card.

Hope deferred makes the heart sick, but a longing fulfilled is a tree of life.

"Oh, Kate. I'm such a terrible person. I threw this verse— well, the first half of it—in Jericho's face weeks ago."

Kate tapped the card. "Okay, so you've lived that first half, but the second part is the promise. That's what you should cling to."

"A longing fulfilled?"

"What are you longing for, Al?"

She licked her lips. "For my family. For us to be together." Her voice came out hushed.

"Tree of life. Sure sounds to me like there's going to be a downpour in the desert." Kate grinned. "I'm going to bed. Don't stay up too much longer."

As Kate's footfalls grew distant, Ali splayed the three cards out in front of her. The empty place in the patch of dirt in her heart could be filled. A tree of life, blossoming with love.

That night, for the first time in eight years, Ali fell asleep full of peace.

The screen door slapped against the back of the house. Ali glanced up from the floor as she mopped.

Megan put up her hands. "Sorry. I didn't know the floor was wet."

Ali leaned the mop against the cabinets. "Don't worry about it. If stuff stays clean for ten seconds around here, I'm amazed." She opened the fridge and pulled out a bottle of water then tossed it to Megan. "I'm sorry I didn't help with classes today. I've got a lot on my mind today."

Megan brushed off the comment with a flick of her wrist, bracelets jingling. "Don't worry about it." She took a sip of the water. "You've got so much going on. Believe me, I'm amazed you haven't said 'enough' and closed the place down."

"I'd never do that. It's too important to me. How did the classes go? Was Hank able to ride for the entire lesson?"

Megan set the bottle of water on the counter. "Yeah, having him lie on the horse with that special saddle was genius. The more contact he has with the horse, the calmer he is."

Ali smiled. "It's the warmth. Hank's tight little muscles against the horse's heated ones loosen him up in a way other physical therapy can't. I'm glad it worked. It's worth the cost of that saddle, then."

Megan nodded. "Bungee's gone lame again, so we won't be able to use him for another week or so. Chance and I mucked the stalls so they're all set for the horses tonight. Do you want me to stick around and help with anything else?"

Ali slipped across the kitchen floor and hugged Megan. "You're amazing. What would I have done without you?"

"Oh, you know." Megan shrugged out of her hug then pointed at the bouquet from Tripp. "Have you sorted out your man problems yet?"

Ali smiled and plucked dead petals from the flowers. "I have. Oh, Megan, I'm in love."

Megan laid a hand on the back of a kitchen chair. "Wow. You made your decision?"

"I did. And I can't believe it took me so long. I mean, he's been so faithful for so many years." The phone rang and Ali grabbed it, reading the caller ID. "Oh, look. It's Tripp. I'm going to take this."

Two days. Too long.

Jericho did a full circle, taking in his childhood home. The lodge-style house did nothing to console him. It stood as a monument for a wealthy man's attempt to feel important. He wanted nothing to do with it.

Pacing, he stepped into the master bedroom. There was a place near the entry to the bathroom where the carpet used to smell like Mom. A bottle of perfume had shattered there, and no matter how many times she scrubbed, the feminine scent lingered. Jericho leaned against the wall and scooted down so he could sit with his hand on the spot.

Wetness gathered in his eyes, so he looked up at the ceiling.

Whenever Pop walloped him good, he'd come here and press his nose into the carpet, remembering his mom. Missing her. Sometimes he'd even tried to talk to her.

But now, more than anything, Jericho wanted Ali. With one last caress of the carpet, he rose to his feet.

He would have walked across their adjoining fields, but the Jeep could bring him there faster. After yanking on his boots, he locked the door and barreled out to his vehicle. Roaring it to life, he sped onto the country road that formed an L around their properties.

He flipped off the music. "Let her call the cops. But she isn't keeping me away any longer."

When he turned onto Ali's property, he rubbed his jaw. He had a brother? It still baffled him. Tripp had tried to use Ali as a tool for revenge. Jericho bit back a growl. How dare Tripp?

He jumped out of the Jeep and crossed to the barn where he figured Ali would be. But he only found Chance tossing a ball to Drover.

"Hiya, Dad!" He trotted over, dog in tow, and flung his arms around Jericho's waist.

"Hey, Chance-man." He squeezed back. "What are you up to?"

His son's shoulders sagged. "Not much. Everyone's upset or crying around here."

"Everyone?"

"Girls. I tell ya." Chance shook his head. "At least Drover's not a girl."

"Has your ma been crying?"

Chance rolled his eyes. "All the time." He chucked the ball at the corral and Drover barked, taking off at high speed. "She said you won't be around anymore, but that I could still spend time with you if I wanted."

"She said that?" Jericho wiped his clammy palms on his jeans.

"Yeah. Guess you made her really sad because she's never not wanted me around, and I do all sorts of dumb things. Did you try saying you're sorry? That usually works. Well, she'll still make you sit in your room for a time-out, but not for that long."

"I'll try to remember that."

"And you don't have a room, so you'd just have to sit on the couch 'cause that's been your bed. It wouldn't be bad because the TV's right there."

"Hear anything else she said about me?"

"Well, she didn't say your name, but the other night she thought I was asleep, and I wasn't. I heard her saying 'I just have to do it' over and over again. Then I *wished* I was sleeping."

A tingle, like ghostly footprints tiptoeing on his skin, walked up his back. *I just have to do it.* But that could only mean...

Jericho gripped the barn door. "Where's your ma, buddy?"

"In the house with Kate and Megan."

"Is it okay with you if I go in there and talk to her about the crying, without you?"

Chance popped the ball out of Drover's mouth. "I don't want anything to do with crying."

Jericho didn't bother with the front door, because the Silvers were always in the kitchen. He came up the back steps and heard Ali talking to someone. He opened the door slowly to prevent the loud slam against the house.

Ali. Pretty Ali. She stood with her back to him, one hand cradling a phone to her ear and the other wrapped around her middle. As he stepped into the kitchen, Megan arched her eyebrows.

Ali played with a magnet on the fridge. "Sure. Tonight would work."

Megan tapped him on the arm. He looked over at her, and she mouthed "Tripp."

It took all his self-control not to storm across the kitchen and wrench the phone from Ali's hand. After everything, she'd entertain a call from the man?

His mind zoomed like an off-road race. *Tonight would work? For what?*

Ali stuck the magnet back in place and walked to the pantry. "I know the place. An hour?" Pause. "Good. It's a date then."

A date? With Tripp?

Jericho jolted back, grabbed the door handle and rushed outside.

Barreling around the house, he heard the back door smack the clapboard, probably leaving a dent. What did he care? Not like anyone wanted him here.

When he was almost to the Jeep, Chance called out. "Hey, Dad! Where are you going? Don't leave."

But he dropped into the driver's seat and slammed the door. Rage poured through his veins. He threw the vehicle into Reverse and made it howl the whole way into town.

Ali set the phone on the counter. "Was that just—did he...?" She raced to the front room in time to see Jericho's Jeep peel out of the driveway.

Kate came down the stairs. "What in the world was that noise?"

"Jericho bolted out of here without talking to me." Ali rubbed her arms. What had he heard? "Can I use the truck, Kate?"

Kate shook her head. "Sorry, sis. I'm already late for work. I need it."

Ali huffed. "Can you drop me off along the way?"

"If it's on the way, then sure. But hurry up."

Ali popped her head into the kitchen. "Megan? Do you mind sticking around and keeping an eye on Chance for a couple hours? I wouldn't ask, but Kate's busy."

Megan tapped her nails on the table. "So you can go on your date?"

"So I can go to dinner, yes."

"You know that's why your husband left. He heard you say 'date,' and he took off like an escaped convict. You can't keep stringing along two men at the same time. There are always consequences."

"I'm not stringing anyone… Oh, can you just watch Chance for me? Yes or no?"

"Love to." Megan smiled.

"Thanks. I owe you big-time."

On Kate's heels, Ali left the house. She bumped into Chance, who was slumped down on the porch steps, palming away tears.

"He left me, Mom. Dad left without talking to me."

Ali gasped and clutched her neck, her heart wrenching as if someone drove a nail through it. She stopped to cradle her son in her arms. Smoothing a hand down his hair, she spoke in a soft tone. "Sweetheart, listen to me. Your father loves you. I want you to keep thinking that while I'm gone. And Chance, I love you, too."

Ali wanted to be angry with Jericho for leaving Chance so upset, but she reminded herself to have patience. He was new to being a father and would learn in time. Besides, if she got her way, Jericho would never leave them again.

Now she just had to locate the man.

Chapter Twenty-Two

Jericho leaned against his Jeep. He scowled at the neon Open sign as the last rays of sun grasped the tips of the mountains. The raucous beat of an old rock song drifted from the door along with wafts of fried food, beer and human sweat. Girls in miniskirts giggled as they sauntered through the entrance together.

He gripped the vehicle's bumper to keep himself from going inside.

One drink. Just one cold, tall lager would ease his mind. Numb the hurt. But one drink would become five. He could embrace sweet escape for one night. But then what? He'd just be back at the start again, with one more mistake to tally against him.

The song switched to a country ballad that baited him to join them inside. He took two steps toward the door and reached for the handle. Then he fisted his hand and paced back to the parking lot.

He'd been so certain they were on the path to reconciling. So sure.

What had Chance said he heard Ali say? I just have to do it. Divorce.

He stomped away from the vehicle, then walked back and

pressed both hands against the side. If she went through with a divorce, then what? Shared custody? Chance for one weekend a month, and three holidays a year? Jericho punched the Jeep.

He wanted to be an everyday part of his son's life. He'd already missed too many milestones. There were so many things he wanted to teach Chance, experiences he wanted to share with the boy. Holidays and weekends wouldn't cut it.

Beyond that, he needed his wife. He longed to hold her against him as they slept, and sit across from her at the dinner table each night. He wanted to do everything in his power to support her chasing after her dreams. But he couldn't do that if she didn't want him.

A truck bumped into the parking lot and stopped a few feet from him.

He glanced over his shoulder. Ali. She looked so pretty that it seared his chest.

She jumped down and waved to Kate. "Don't worry about picking me up. Jericho will take me home." Ali sashayed toward him. "Hey, stranger." She beamed.

He glanced at the bar, then back at Ali. His shoulders sagged. She'd come looking for him at the bar, and he'd proved her assumptions right. Why was she even here?

She snatched his hand as she came near. "Grab some curb with me?"

They sat down, and she scooted closer. Her legs touched his, and their shoulders in contact made every inch on that side of his body burn. He reminded himself to take a breath. "Aren't you going to be late for your date?"

"Naw." She turned his wrist over, tapping the watch. "I still have thirty minutes."

The wind picked up and her scent wrapped around him, tempting him more than any bottle of beer ever could. Yet he couldn't have this woman.

His eyes started to sting. "I didn't go inside."

"I know." She captured his chin and turned his face to look

her in the eye. "I believe you. I trust you. Hear that, Jericho Freed? I know you'll never touch the stuff again."

"But you knew to look for me here." He snaked away from her, hiding his face in his hands.

"Sure. You're human. You'll always be tempted, but I know you're too strong to give in." She bumped her shoulder into his. "So why the long face?"

Jericho studied the gravel at his feet and steepled his hands. "Are you gonna divorce me?"

"Why would I go and do a fool thing like that?"

He swung his head toward her. His mouth went dry. "You're not going to sign any papers?"

Her lips pulled up slowly. "That would make it a whole lot harder to be married to you if I did. And being married to you is what I want most of all." She looped her arm through his. "It just took me a while to realize it."

"Talk straight to me, woman."

She turned and framed his face with her hands, pulling their heads so they were inches apart. "Listen to me. I love you, Jericho Freed. You're the only man who's ever been in my heart." She bit one side of her lip, and her eyebrows darted up. "Straight enough?"

His heart started up like a hoof kicking his chest. He searched her face. The gold flecks in her eyes shimmered. He'd never seen anything more stunning. Incapable of stopping himself, he leaned down and brushed his lips against hers.

Not wanting to startle her, he moved to break the moment, but she brought her arms around his neck. Pulling herself against him, she deepened the kiss, her lips warm and melding to his. He sifted her soft hair through his fingers. His hands explored the curve of her neck and traveled down her spine.

When they parted, a chuckle rumbled in his chest. She

leaned her forehead against his, and their eyes locked like partners in a dance. Ali had a goofy grin pulling at her cheeks.

"I love you, Ali Silver."

"Ali Freed. I'm going to change it back. Has a nice ring to it." She sighed, lacing her fingers through his. Her head rested against his shoulder.

"Ali Freed. I do like the sound of that." He stiffened, sitting straighter. "Okay, but then I don't understand why you're going on a date with Tripp."

Her eyes widened. "That's why I'm here. I want you to come with me."

"On a date with him?"

"No. I only said yes because I want to confront him. But I'm afraid of what he'll do if you're not beside me. After everything he's done, I can't trust him. Will you come?"

He tucked her hair behind her ear. "I'd go to Africa right now with you if you asked."

"Do you think you can face him after everything you found out?"

"You mean since learning he's my brother?"

"Yes. Do you know for sure if that's true?"

He nodded. "I talked to Pop, and he confirmed it. It's wild. I'm half pleased to know I have another relation in the world, but the other half of me wants to kill him for what he's put you through."

She rose, offering her hand. He took it and stood, but then tugged her to a stop. "Hey. I wasn't after you for the money, either. You know that, right?"

"It wouldn't matter even if you were. I love you and want to be with you, so we'd both win."

Jericho clutched her shoulders and gave a small shake. "It matters to me." He led her to the Jeep. "I knew nothing about that will until the other morning. And I could care less about the ranch and Pop's money."

"What about the bank stuff?"

"I did have meetings with the bank, and I have set up a business. It's a little nonprofit operation, and I'm hoping you'll consent to helping me get it up and running."

"A nonprofit?"

"Yes. It's tentatively named A Soldier's Dream, but if you don't like it, we can change that. I'd like to couple it with Big Sky Dreams and offer therapeutic horseback riding for injured soldiers and for soldiers' spouses while they're overseas."

Ali screamed. She hugged him so tight his back cracked.

"Jericho! That's the greatest idea I've ever heard. I'm already certified to do that. We can start classes right away. I'll have to do a little bit of research and plan different lessons."

He smiled down at her as she rattled off information, loving the way her lips moved over the words. "Whoa there, sweetheart. I still have to finish filling out paperwork with the government so we can be recognized as an approved program for servicemen. Then I want to join our companies and help with all the expenses. Add horses to the program, maybe another arena and riding barn."

Her face fell. "That's a lot of money."

He shrugged. "I have enough."

"But how? I don't think the army pays an injured vet a lot of money, and I know you haven't been working anywhere since coming home."

"My mom had a separate will. Hers stipulated that my father didn't get a dime of her money. Instead, it was held in an account until my twenty-first birthday, when the totality of the funds became available to me. The only problem was, I didn't have a clue. Pop never told me. When I got back in town, Mom's lawyer contacted me. I couldn't believe he hadn't retired yet. It took a lot of paperwork, but the funds are now free and clear and mine."

"I thought your dad was the rich one."

"Me, too. But I guess they basically had an arranged marriage. Their parents were business partners. The Freeds had land but were low on money, and the Austers had money but no land. So they merged."

"Do you think she did it because she was angry with your father?"

Jericho opened the door and ushered her inside. She climbed up, and he stood in the open area, drinking in the sight of her. He sighed. "Yes. I think she knew he cheated, and that's why she changed her will. I'm sure she justified her actions because she was angry."

She put a hand on his forearm. "Bitterness can do that to a person."

"I love you, Ali."

"I know. Now get your hide in action, or we'll be late."

Unable to resist, Jericho kissed her cheek before closing the door. Her giggle worked its way into all the broken places in his heart.

With her hand clasped in Jericho's, Ali walked into the restaurant and spotted Tripp. "Let me do most of the talking," she whispered.

When she stiffened, Jericho slipped his arm around her shoulders and pressed his lips close to her ear. "Did I ever tell you you're the perfect height?"

She swatted at him, but her smile fell when she met Tripp's gaze. The lawyer's mouth pulled into a grim line as he rose. "Well, I asked you here to give you my side of the story, but I see you've decided which man you trust."

Jericho tensed. Ali gave his side a squeeze and sat down. She folded her hands on top of the linen tablecloth. "I'd like to give you the benefit of the doubt, Tripp. I've learned the dangers of jumping to conclusions." Her eyes darted to Jericho, and her husband's lips tugged to a whisper of a smile, but the crease in his brow stated his true mood.

Tripp pulled at his collar. "This is going to be awkward saying everything in front of him." He gestured to Jericho.

Ali laid a hand on her husband's arm. "Jericho and I are a package deal. It's your choice. Talk to both of us, or neither."

Tripp raked a hand through his hair. A shock of it fell forward onto his forehead. "All right. I knew about the will. I've known about it since the day I started my internship with Jeb Strong. But you have to understand, Alison, I'm not an ogre."

"Did you slash my tires? Did you kill Denny?"

Tripp's eyebrows shot up. "No. Absolutely not. I care about you. That's what I'm trying to say. I'd never do anything like that to hurt you. I admit, I saw the will and realized the loophole—that if you married me, and I legally adopted Chance, then when Abram passed away, I'd stand to inherit everything."

"You would have faked a marriage with me?" In an effort to draw strength from Jericho's touch, Ali groped for his hand under the table. His strong fingers closed around hers. His thumb traced a pattern on the back of her fist.

"No, nothing like that. You've been a good friend to me for years, Alison. I don't have many people in my life who genuinely care about me. Our friendship means a lot. I care about your well-being. I know you've been hurt deeply, and I would have been an honest and faithful husband to you. It killed me seeing Chance without a father when I would have gladly stepped into that role." He toyed with the coffee mug on the table. "You see, I know how terrible it is being a boy without a dad. I didn't want that for him. I thought I was doing something noble, but you're looking at me like I'm the leftovers from gutting a deer."

"Not when you put it like that. You're a good man, Tripp. You'll be an amazing husband to the right girl, and a devoted father." She leaned over and squeezed his hand.

"I'm not a monster," he whispered. "My mother and I, we really struggled. Dinner wasn't a daily event, if you catch my drift. She told me I wasn't allowed to tell anyone Abram was my father. Said it would shame her. But after she died, I confronted him." He let go of the mug and looked up. "How do you think I made it through college and law school debt-free?"

Jericho leaned forward. "That still doesn't explain why you would send a threatening letter to Ali and then sabotage stuff around the ranch."

"I didn't."

"He's right, Jericho. It's clear now. Rider did it all along."

Tripp swirled the water in his glass. "No. Rider Longley's innocent as a pastor on Sunday."

Ali gasped. "But you helped me fire him."

"I hadn't figured it out yet. Everything finally clicked this morning, or I would have told you sooner. It's that girl you have working with you, Megan Galveen."

Ali reached for her purse under the table. "No way. I can't believe that. Megan is my friend. She's helped us above and beyond what I expect from her on many occasions."

Jericho cleared his throat. "And what would her motive be? Didn't the letter say something about seeing me and Ali together at the Independence Day picnic? Why would she care about us?"

Tripp closed his eyes. "No. It's me. She's after me."

Ali yanked the crumpled threat letter from her purse, smoothing it on the table. "It doesn't say your name, Jericho. I just assumed it meant you. But it could mean Tripp. She could have seen him walking me away at the picnic. She may have meant stay away from Tripp."

Tripp nodded. He scanned the note. "That *is* what it means. I wish you had shown this to me because I received a couple of these glued magazine cutout letters, too."

"But she's never said anything. You honestly think she did all those things?" Ali rubbed her hands back and forth over the tablecloth.

"Think about it. She has access to your bank account for Big Sky Dreams, and money keeps disappearing."

Jericho jolted. "Her father works at the Mountaintop Research Laboratory. Her sister told me when I got my loan. They mess around with real heavy-duty drugs for bioterrorism purposes."

Tears rushed to Ali's eyes. "Denny."

Jericho reached over and stroked her hair.

Tripp drummed the table. "She's been stalking me since they came to town. At first I was flattered, and I'll admit I used her to gain information about you. That's how I knew about your loan, Jericho." He rubbed his jaw. "But then the letters started, and she kept showing up wherever I would be. She crossed the line when she showed up in my house in just her robe last night. I went to the police at that point to document everything." Tripp unbuckled his briefcase and pulled out a file. "The detective I worked with looked into her past. That's what's in this file." He pushed the manila envelope toward Jericho.

Jericho pawed through the papers, a deep scowl marring his face.

Tripp pulled out one of the reports. "Scary reading. She fell in love with her high school math teacher and become obsessive. She ended up tinkering with the engine of his wife's car. It caused an accident. The man's wife suffered massive injuries. Megan did a stint in juvie for it. She's also been arrested in another case for stalking and violating a restraining order. There's an incident of battery where she attacked the girlfriend of a man she liked, too."

Ali's pulse pounded in her throat. She shoved to her feet, hands shaking. "Chance."

Jericho touched her elbow. "Ali, what's wrong?"

"Chance is at the house with Megan. She thought I had a date with Tripp." She grabbed Jericho's shoulder. "We have to go. She could hurt him. He trusts her completely." Tears rushed to Ali's eyes. "If something happens to Chance, I'll never forgive myself."

Chapter Twenty-Three

Jericho stayed zoned to the road. His Jeep's headlights tore through the darkness. Tripp's car trailed their bumper by inches.

The wheels smacked into a pothole, jarring Ali's spine. "What if she does something to him? He's so vulnerable. What if he's hurt?"

Jericho's hand shot out and clasped hers. "Pray with me, Ali. God, protect our son."

Rounding the bend, an orange glow sliced through the onyx sky. Ali squinted. Across the fields, mammoth flames licked the underbelly of heaven. Smoke traced puffy fingers up into the stars.

Reality struck like a sucker punch.

Her throat clogged. She grabbed Jericho's arm. "Fire."

Flames consumed the ranch house. Splashes of lava-orange and sunburst-yellow erupted, ravaging everything but the structure's skeleton, which stood a somber black against the blazing backlight. Smoke burned in the air as a million glowing ashes hung suspended, eerie lightning bugs in the gloom. The fire leaped from the building, devouring the hay and feed piles in the yard, spilling over into the corral.

A swarm of firefighters and police officers filled the driveway. The lights from their emergency vehicles bounced blue and red off the barn.

Wrenching open the door, Ali jumped from the still-moving vehicle. "Chance!" A sob choked her as she shoved past the rescue workers. Ali fought against the waves of heat rolling from the house.

An iron arm seized her waist and jerked her backward. "Ali. No." Jericho dragged her away from the inferno.

With a moan, the structure's roof caved. Ali screamed.

Fighting him, she yelled over the roaring flames. "Let me go! I have to save him. He could be burning to death in there. Chance! Let me go." She kicked, trying to twist from his unyielding grasp.

Jericho spun her to face him, chin jutting out. "No. You're not going in there. I'll go in. It doesn't matter if I get hurt. But he needs you."

Jericho set her back a step and elbowed through a group of firefighters lugging a hose. Jericho bent to charge into the fire, but an officer stopped him.

Ali bit her nails. She blinked, trying to see the house through the haze and her tears.

The police officer approached with Jericho. "Are you the home owner, miss?"

Ali latched onto the man's arm. "Our son. I think he's in the house. Please let us go in. We have to save him."

The cop's eyes softened. "Let me guess, a freckled thing about yea high who can talk the wheels off a wheelbarrow?"

Jericho looped his arm around Ali's waist. "Sounds about right."

"He's safe. Follow me."

Leaving behind the unholy music of crackling fire, splitting boards and crumbling dreams, they stepped toward three police cruisers parked near the barn.

The breath whooshed out of Ali's lungs when Chance raced around the last car and bounded toward them. "Mom! Dad!"

She dropped to her knees, and Chance launched into her arms. Rocking back and forth, she wept into his hair. "I love you so much."

Jericho's arms encircled both of them, pulling his family against his chest. He rubbed at his own glistening eyes. "I love you both. Thank God you're okay."

Chance trembled in her arms. "Our house. Mom, our house is gone."

She stroked his back. "I know, sweetheart. But it's not important. You're safe. That's all that matters to us."

The police officer cleared his throat. "I'll need some statements from you folks."

Ali coughed. "I don't understand. How did you know to come here?"

Chance pushed back against her. "That's easy, Mom. They followed Rider."

"What does Rider have to do with this?"

Her son pointed his thumb in the direction of the ambulance. "He's over there."

She rose, Jericho and Chance right behind her. Ali rounded the ambulance to where Rider sat under a paramedic's steady hand. His face was a patchwork of soot as rivulets of sweat carved paths that dripped from his jaw. He'd lost his tell-tale hat, so his hair fell damp and tangled on his forehead. His button-up and jeans were torn and charred, with a burnt hole where fire had tried to nip at his chest.

The cowboy straightened. "Miss Ali, I know I'm not supposed to be on your property, but I ran into Kate at the town square and she told me what's been going on. I got to thinking that Megan was always around when bad things happened. And some of the things she'd told me didn't line up right with what Kate said. When she told me Chance was here, I called the cops and—" he shrugged "—seems they already knew her name and about some trouble in her past, so they were quick to follow me. I hope you aren't upset that I disobeyed you about staying clear of your property."

Ali reached out and placed her hand on his arm. She locked eyes before he could dip his chin. "You saved my son's life. How can I ever thank you?"

"Can I have my job back?"

She engulfed him in a tight hug, her head buried against his neck. "Of course. I'm so sorry I doubted you."

Jericho placed a hand on her shoulder. "Did you go in the fire after our boy? Is that how you got burned?"

Chance stepped between his parents, tears dried, ready to be the center of attention. "Oh, no. It wasn't on fire yet when he came for me."

Ali squinted at Chance through the fading light. "*Yet?* What happened?"

Her son leaned against the ambulance's bumper. "Megan said we were going to play cowboys and Indians. She said I could only be the cowboy if she got to tie me up. But she said not to worry because cowboys are strong and can get out of the knots. So I let her, and she went outside to do a rain dance. I reminded her that we got a bunch of rain the other day. But she still went out, and I saw her walking around the house for a long time. I don't think she did the dance right though, because it smelled like a gas station instead of rain."

Ali gasped. Jericho's grip tightened.

Chance rambled on. "And she was wrong about the ropes, because I couldn't get them off. And I really tried. Maybe if I didn't have a cast? But then Rider came in and said it wasn't a good game to play. He brought me to Denny's stall and told me to stay hidden."

Tears rolled down Ali's cheeks as she turned to Rider. "Then how did you get burned?"

"When I came out of the barn, Megan had torched the house, and I saw her run inside. Don't know about you, Miss Ali, but I don't believe even the worst of folks deserve a fate like that. Couldn't have lived with myself if I hadn't gone in after her."

Chance patted Rider's leg. "He should enter the calf wrestling contest at the next rodeo. I think he'd win. He pulled Megan outside and she tried to get away, but Rider took her down in four seconds flat. Even with her biting him."

"Hush, Chance." Rider grunted. "I'm not getting my chest all puffed up over tackling a lady."

Ali met Rider's gaze. "But I thought you hated us."

"Are you talking about that lawsuit, Miss Ali?"

She nodded.

"I'm not a part of that. I don't have a thing against you. My older sisters are suing you. They're stuck in the past, in that moment when our parents died. They're so bitter. They can't let go." He rubbed his palms back and forth on his jeans. "But I've never agreed with them. It wasn't your fault that the truck hit them. Never was. That's why they call it an accident. I'm trying to talk them into dropping their fool vendetta. It's hotheaded. Nothing can bring our parents back."

Ali paced away from the men. Her gaze landed on the hissing leftovers of her home. Her hand clapped over her mouth.

Anger and being unwilling to forgive could bring such destruction. Granting bitterness reign caused heartache. Her own mother, Jericho's mother, Megan and Rider's sisters all stood testament to it. And she had almost been like that, too.

The gravel crunched as Jericho stepped up beside her. He opened his arms.

She leaned against him. "What are we going to do?"

He kissed her forehead. "Rebuild. You and Chance are safe. That's all that matters to me. We'll clear this rubble and build a new home. A fresh start, together. That is, if you'll have me?"

Ali rested her hands on his chest, smoothing her thumbs against the fabric. She tipped up her eyes, her voice husky. "Are you asking what I think you are?"

His eyebrow rose. "Need me to go down on one knee?"

"I'd rather you keep holding me."

His arms tightened. "Ali, I love you. Let me be beside you for the rest of my life. Raise our son together. Marry me, again?"

Little hands shoved against their legs. "What are you guys doing?"

Ali laughed. "Your dad's asking me to marry him."

Chance scrunched his face. "But you can't, Mom."

She met Jericho's alarmed look and winked. "Why not, buddy?"

He rolled his eyes. "'Cause it's silly. You're already married."

Jericho placed a hand on their son's head. "The kid does have a point."

Ali turned in Jericho's arms as Tripp approached. She smiled at him.

He stopped a few feet away, shifting his weight from one foot to the other. He kicked at the gravel. "I took the liberty of speaking with the police and giving them a detailed account of all that's happened at the ranch. I hope I didn't miss anything. They'll require a written statement from you tomorrow, but you're free to go tonight. They're transferring Megan to the county jail tomorrow. I suggested a psychological examination."

"Thank you for taking care of that, Tripp."

He slipped his hands into his pockets. "I guess I'll be off, then."

Breaking free of Jericho, Ali touched Tripp's forearm. "I want you to know that you're always welcome on my property. I understand why you did what you did, and I appreciate what you were willing to be for Chance."

"No problem."

Tripp started to turn, but she stopped him. "If it's not too much to ask, I still want you to be a part of his life."

She looked over her shoulder at Chance and Jericho. Her son leaned against his father. Jericho had his arms looped around their boy.

She looked Tripp in the eye. "I mean, you're his uncle, after all."

"You'd let me be a part of his life like that? After everything?"

"Yes, Tripp. Please, be part of our family?"

He pressed a hand against his face. "I've never— No one's ever—"

Jericho cleared his throat. "I'll be needing some lawyer advice from you, too."

Tripp's gaze darted between Jericho and Ali.

"Seems that someday I'm going to be left a heap of property that I don't need, or want. See, I'm planning to build a house right here for my family. But this property that's coming to me in a will, well, I'd like to make sure that I can legally pass it to my brother. Think you can help me?"

Tripp's jaw dropped. He worked to close it, then opened it again. "If you're sure?"

Jericho draped an arm around Ali and snaked the other one around Chance. "I'm sure."

"Then, in a legal sense, I think I might be able to help you. Thank you. I'm not really sure what to say."

"And like Ali said, I'd be proud if you'd be Chance's uncle."

Tripp blinked a couple times, looked at the ground then nodded.

As the last of the fire engines and police squad cars rolled off her property, Ali batted her hand against the smell of smoke in the air. She couldn't look at the rubble that had once been her childhood home.

Jericho slipped a cell phone into her hand. "Call your sister. Tell her not to come here tonight."

She took the phone, but didn't use it. Ali wrapped her arms around her middle. "But where will we go?"

"My dad's house is across the ridge, and I plan on bringing my family home there tonight, if that's fine by you." Jericho trailed a finger down her cheek.

She reached for his hand and pressed a kiss to his palm. "It's fine by me. I'll call Kate and let her know to meet us there."

Chance latched onto Jericho's hand. "We're going to live in your house now?"

"Only for a little while. We're going to build a new house with plenty of room for all your sisters and brothers." He winked at Ali.

She tossed back her head and laughed.

Chance bolted ahead in the field and spun around, Drover leaping behind him. "First a dad, then an uncle, and now sisters and brothers? Whoa. This family is getting huge!"

Tree of life. Ali smiled.

She laced her fingers with Jericho's and they walked across the field, whispering their dreams to each other as Chance and Drover ran ahead.

* * * * *

Dear Reader,

Do you ever feel like God is far from you? I know I've felt that way before. Ali sure did.

Because of all the bad that happened in her life Ali assumed that God walked away from her. In the end, she faces a choice. She can stay hidden behind her wall of bitterness and be alone, or she can find hope in forgiveness. I'm so glad she chose the latter.

Life is hard. It's easy to let difficult emotions and struggles consume us. Ali pictures God slamming the door of her heart and yelling, "Enough!" as He walks away. But she was wrong. God was with her the whole time, waiting for her to come back to Him.

If you feel far from God, I pray you will take the chance now to return to Him. I promise He's strong enough for whatever you are facing today.

Thank you for reading Ali and Jericho's story. They've lived in my heart for the past two years. I'm tickled to see them finally on paper. I love interacting with readers on Facebook. Look up my author page and say hi!

Much love,
Jessica Keller

Questions for Discussion

1. Ali has understandable reasons to be angry and bitter toward Jericho. Did you find Ali's transformation believable or not? How come?

2. Ali keeps Chance's parentage a secret because she's afraid Jericho's still dangerous. Do you think this was right or wrong of her? Is there ever a situation where deception is acceptable? What are some stories in the Bible that include deception?

3. Jericho feels that God told him to go home and fix his marriage. Ali shoves him away at every turn, and Jericho starts to wonder if he heard God wrong. Have you ever had a strong feeling that God wanted you to do something but found all sorts of obstacles in your path? Jericho presses through the obstacles and wins back his wife. Have you ever felt God wanted you to do something specific? Were you able to accomplish that, and if not, what changed your mind?

4. Kate tells Ali that she holds all the power because Jericho asked for forgiveness. What do you think Kate meant by this? Do you think it's true that forgiveness gives us power?

5. Because of his father's stroke, Jericho will never receive an apology for how he was mistreated when he was a child. Jericho has to learn to forgive his father without knowing if his father is truly sorry. We all have people who have wronged us in our lives. When was the last time you forgave someone when they didn't deserve or ask for it? Is there someone in your life like this right now?

6. Instead of going straight to the police when she receives a threatening letter, Ali tries to solve the problem herself. She could have been saved a lot of grief if she would have asked for help, but not having police assistance afforded her and Jericho time to bond that might not have happened otherwise. Have you ever attempted to manage a problem on your own that got out of hand? Do you wish you had sought help, or are you glad with the end result?

7. Jericho tells Ali that she's made her horse, Denny, into her savior. What did he mean by this? Have your priorities ever gotten out of whack? What happened to set them right again?

8. For the past eight years, Ali assumed God had abandoned her, but on her camping trip she realizes that she's the one who walked away from God. This one moment changes Ali's life. Can you point to an "Aha!" moment or a perspective shift that had the same impact on you? What was it? What were the circumstances surrounding it?

9. Ali is afraid that if she darkens the door to a church, God will send lightning bolts at her, but when she finally attends, she's greeted warmly by friends who have missed her. Have you had a similar experience where you were expected to be treated one way and found grace instead? What were the circumstances? How did other people's unexpected reactions impact you?

10. In the story, Ali's mother and Rider's sisters are eaten up with bitterness. It stops them from moving on after tragedies. Have you ever experienced something like this? How difficult was it to let go of bitterness?

11. Jericho loves his wife and goes out of his way to show her. In what ways did Jericho's love for Ali resemble God's love for us?

12. Tripp says he's making a noble choice when he offers to adopt Chance and marry Ali. Given his past, do you believe he's sincere?

13. In the end, Jericho and Ali invite Tripp to be a part of their family. Does this seem like a wise choice? What would you have done?

14. If you could write an epilogue, what hurdles, if any, do you see in Jericho and Ali's future? What do you imagine would happen to Kate, Tripp and Rider?

REQUEST YOUR FREE BOOKS!

2 FREE INSPIRATIONAL NOVELS
PLUS 2
FREE
MYSTERY GIFTS

Love Inspired®

*With her own business in a fledgling frontier town,
Cassie Godfrey will be self-sufficient at last. But her
solitary plans are interrupted by four young orphans—
and one persistent cowboy.*

Read on for a sneak peek of
THE COWBOY'S UNEXPECTED FAMILY *by Linda Ford.*

"How long do you think it will take to contact the children's uncle?"

"I wouldn't venture a guess. Why? You already wishing I was gone?"

"You make me sound rude and ungrateful. I'm not. I just have plans. Goals. Don't you?"

Roper stared off in the distance for a moment, his expression uncharacteristically serious. Then he flashed Cassie a teasing grin. "Now that you mention it, I guess I don't. Apart from making sure the kids are safe."

"I find that hard to believe. Don't you want to get your own ranch?"

Roper shrugged, his smile never faltering. "Don't mind being free to go where I want, work for the man I wish to work for."

"Wouldn't you like to have a family of your own?"

"I never think of family. Never had any, except for the other kids in the orphanage." He laughed. "An odd sort of family, I guess. No roots. Changing with the seasons."

Cassie didn't know how to respond to his description of family. With no response coming to her mind, she shifted back to her concern. "Roper, about our arrangement. I—"

He chuckled. "I know what you're going to say, but this isn't about you or me. It's about the kids."

"So long as you remember that."

"I aim to. I got rules, you know. Like never stay where you're not wanted. Don't put down roots you'll likely have ripped out."

She guessed there was a story behind his last statement. Likely something he'd learned by bitter experience. "I plan to put down roots right here." She jabbed her finger toward the ground.

"That's the difference between you and me." The grin remained on his lips, but she noticed it didn't reach his eyes.

Whispers and giggles came from behind the wooden walls. "Do you think the children will be okay?"

"You did good in telling them they'll be safe here." His grin seemed to be both approving and teasing.

"They will be safe as much as it lies within me to make it so." And they'd never be made to feel like they were burdens. Not if Cassie had anything to do with it.

*Don't miss THE COWBOY'S UNEXPECTED FAMILY
by Linda Ford, the next book in the
COWBOYS OF EDEN VALLEY series,
available March 2013 from Love Inspired Historical!*

LIEXP0213